## Purple Lilac:
*Love's First Emotions*

One look into Ky Silver's
sea-green eyes had evoked
love's first stirrings. Ky had
been her first lover, and
Kate Hardesty had fallen hook,
line and sinker. But she'd
walked out on him all those
years ago. Now she was back—
could she handle Ky the second
time around?

# NORA ROBERTS
### LANGUAGE OF LOVE

Love has a language all its own, and for
centuries, flowers have symbolized
love's finest expression.
Discover the language of flowers
—and love—
in this romantic collection of 48 favorite
books by bestselling author Nora Roberts.

1. Lily of the Valley
   IRISH THOROUGHBRED
2. Hollyhock THE LAW IS A LADY
3. Cabbage Rose IRISH ROSE
4. Wallflower STORM WARNING
5. Foxglove FIRST IMPRESSIONS
6. Yellow Jasmine REFLECTIONS
7. Marigold NIGHT MOVES
8. Narcissus DANCE OF DREAMS
9. China Aster OPPOSITES ATTRACT
10. Amaryllis ISLAND OF FLOWERS
11. Great Yellow Daffodil
    SEARCH FOR LOVE
12. Hyacinth PLAYING THE ODDS
13. Gloxinia TEMPTING FATE
14. Forget-me-not FROM THIS DAY
15. Petunia ALL THE POSSIBILITIES
16. Tuberose THE HEART'S VICTORY
17. Red Poppy ONE MAN'S ART
18. Gladiola RULES OF THE GAME
19. White Periwinkle
    FOR NOW, FOREVER
20. Pansy HER MOTHER'S KEEPER
21. Orchid PARTNERS
22. Stock SULLIVAN'S WOMAN
23. Dahlia SUMMER DESSERTS
24. Iris THIS MAGIC MOMENT
25. Pink LESSONS LEARNED
26. Lavender THE RIGHT PATH
27. Love in a Mist
    THE ART OF DECEPTION
28. Azalea UNTAMED
29. Red Carnation DUAL IMAGE
30. Bluebell SECOND NATURE
31. Red and White Roses
    ONE SUMMER
32. Wisteria GABRIEL'S ANGEL
33. Trumpet Flower
    THE NAME OF THE GAME
34. Purple Columbine
    A WILL AND A WAY
35. Honeysuckle AFFAIRE ROYALE
36. Spring Crocus
    LESS OF A STRANGER
37. Crown Imperial
    COMMAND PERFORMANCE
38. White Camellia BLITHE IMAGES
39. Cyclamen THE PLAYBOY PRINCE
40. Purple Lilac TREASURES LOST,
    TREASURES FOUND
41. White Daisy RISKY BUSINESS
42. Red Tulip LOVING JACK
43. Apple Blossom TEMPTATION
44. Dogwood BEST LAID PLANS
45. Clematis MIND OVER MATTER
46. Garden Anemone THE WELCOMING
47. Snapdragon BOUNDARY LINES
48. Morning Glory LOCAL HERO

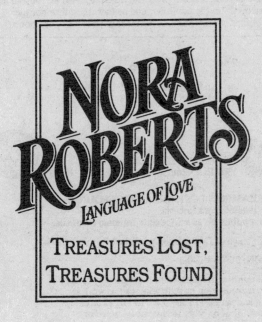

# NORA ROBERTS

## LANGUAGE OF LOVE

# TREASURES LOST, TREASURES FOUND

## Silhouette Books

Published by Silhouette Books New York

**America's Publisher of Contemporary Romance**

To Dixie Browning,
the true lady of the island

**SILHOUETTE BOOKS**
300 East 42nd St., New York, N.Y. 10017

TREASURES LOST, TREASURES FOUND
© 1986 by Nora Roberts.
First published as a Silhouette Intimate Moments.

Language of Love edition published February 1994.

ISBN: 0-373-51040-3

Printed in U.S.A.

# Chapter One

He had believed in it. Edwin J. Hardesty hadn't been the kind of man who had fantasies or followed dreams, but sometime during his quiet, literary life he had looked for a pot of gold. From the information in the reams of notes, the careful charts and the dog-eared research books, he thought he'd found it.

In the panelled study, a single light shot a beam across a durable oak desk. The light fell over a hand—narrow, slender, without the affectation of rings or polish. Yet even bare, it remained an essentially feminine hand, the kind that could be pictured holding a porcelain cup or waving a feather fan. It was a surprisingly elegant hand for a woman who didn't consider herself elegant, delicate or particularly feminine. Kathleen Hardesty was, as her father had been, and as he'd directed her to be, a dedicated educator.

Minds were her concern—the expanding and the fulfilling of them. This included her own as well as every one of her students'. For as long as she could remember, her father had impressed upon her the importance of education. He'd stressed the priority of it over every other aspect of life. Education was the cohesiveness that held civilization together. She grew up surrounded by the dusty smell of books and the quiet, placid tone of patient instruction.

She'd been expected to excel in school, and she had. She'd been expected to follow her father's path into education. At twenty-eight, Kate was just finishing her first year at Yale as an assistant professor of English literature.

In the dim light of the quiet study, she looked the part. Her light brown hair was tidily secured at the nape of her neck with all the pins neatly tucked in. Her practical tortoiseshell reading glasses seemed dark against her milk-pale complexion. Her high cheekbones gave her face an almost haughty look that was often dispelled by her warm, doe-brown eyes.

Though her jacket was draped over the back of her chair, the white blouse she wore was still crisp. Her cuffs were turned back to reveal delicate wrists and a slim Swiss watch on her left arm. Her earrings were tasteful gold studs given to Kate by her father on her twenty-first birthday, the only truly personal gift she could ever remember receiving from him.

Seven long years later, one short week after her father's funeral, Kate sat at his desk. The room still carried the scent of his cologne and a hint of the pipe tobacco he'd only smoked in that room.

She'd finally found the courage to go through his papers.

She hadn't known he was ill. In his early sixties, Hardesty had looked robust and strong. He hadn't told his daughter about his visits to the doctor, his check-ups, ECG results or the little pills he carried with him everywhere. She'd found his pills in his inside pocket after his fatal heart attack. Kate hadn't known his heart was weak because Hardesty never shared his shortcomings with anyone. She hadn't known about the charts and research papers in his desk; he'd never shared his dreams either.

Now that she was aware of both, Kate wasn't certain she ever really knew the man who'd raised her. The memory of her mother was dim; that was to be expected after more than twenty years. Her father had been alive just a week before.

Leaning back for a moment, she pushed her glasses up and rubbed the bridge of her nose between her thumb and forefinger. She tried, with only the desk lamp between herself and the dark, to think of her father in precise terms.

Physically, he'd been a tall, big man with a full head of steel-gray hair and a patient face. He had favored dark suits and white shirts. The only vanity she could remember had been his weekly manicures. But it wasn't a physical picture Kate struggled with now. As a father...

He was never unkind. In all her memories, Kate couldn't remember her father ever raising his voice to her, ever striking her. He never had to, she thought with a sigh. All he had to do was express disappointment, disapproval, and that was enough.

He had been brilliant, tireless, dedicated. But all of that had been directed toward his vocation. As a father, Kate reflected...He'd never been unkind. That was all that would come to her, and because of it she felt a fresh wave of guilt and grief.

She hadn't disappointed him, that much she could cling to. He had told her so himself, in just those words, when she was accepted by the English Department at Yale. Nor had he expected her ever to disappoint him. Kate knew, though it had never been discussed, that her father wanted her to become head of the English Department within ten years. That had been the extent of his dream for her.

Had he ever realized just how much she'd loved him? She wondered as she shut her eyes, tired now from the hours of reading her father's handwriting. Had he ever known just how desperately she'd wanted to please him? If he'd just once said he was proud...

In the end, she hadn't had those few intense last moments with her father one reads about in books or sees in the movies. When she'd arrived at the hospital, he was already gone. There'd been no time for words. No time for tears.

Now she was on her own in the tidy Cape Cod house she'd shared with him for so long. The housekeeper would still come on Wednesday mornings, and the gardener would come on Saturdays to cut the grass. She alone would have to deal with the paperwork, the sorting, the shifting, the clearing out.

That could be done. Kate leaned back further in her father's worn leather chair. It could be done because all of those things were practical matters. She dealt easily with the practical. But what about these papers she'd found? What would she do about the carefully drawn charts, the notebooks filled with information, directions, history, theory? In part, because she was raised to be logical, she considered filing them neatly away.

But there was another part, the part that enabled one to lose oneself in fantasies, in dreams, in the "perhapses" of life. This was the part that allowed Kate to lose herself totally in the possibilities of the written word, in the wonders of a book. The papers on her father's desk beckoned her.

He'd believed in it. She bent over the papers again. He'd believed in it or he never would have wasted his time documenting, searching, theorizing. She would never be able to discuss it with him. Yet, in a way, wasn't he telling her about it through his words?

Treasure. Sunken treasure. The stuff of fiction and Hollywood movies. Judging by the stack of papers and notebooks on his desk, Hardesty must have spent months, perhaps years, compiling information on the location of an English merchant ship lost off the coast of North Carolina two centuries before.

It brought Kate an immediate picture of Edward Teach—Blackbeard, the bloodthirsty pirate with the crazed superstitions and reign of terror. The stuff of romances, she thought. Of romance...

Ocracoke Island. The memory was sharp, sweet and painful. Kate had blocked out everything that had happened that summer four years before. Everything and everyone. Now, if she was to make a rational decision about what was to be done, she had to think of those long, lazy months on the remote Outer Banks of North Carolina.

She'd begun work on her doctorate. It had been a surprise when her father had announced that he planned to spend the summer on Ocracoke and invited her to accompany him. Of course, she'd gone, taking her portable typewriter, boxes of books, reams of paper. She hadn't expected to be seduced by white sand beaches and the call of gulls. She hadn't expected to fall desperately and insensibly in love.

Insensibly, Kate repeated to herself, as if in defense. She'd have to remember that was the most apt adjective. There'd been nothing sensible about her feelings for Ky Silver.

Even the name, she mused, was unique, unconventional, flashy. They'd been as suitable for each other as a peacock and a wren. Yet that hadn't stopped her from losing her head, her heart and her innocence during that balmy, magic summer.

She could still see him at the helm of the boat her father had rented, steering into the wind, laughing, dark hair flowing wildly. She could still remember that heady, weightless feeling when they'd gone scuba diving in the warm coastal waters. Kate had been too caught up in what was happening to herself to think about her father's sudden interest in boating and diving.

She'd been too swept away by her own feelings of astonishment that a man like Ky Silver should be attracted to someone like her to notice her father's preoccupation with currents and tides. There'd been too much excitement for her to realize that her father never bothered with fishing rods like the other vacationers.

But now her youthful fancies were behind her, Kate told herself. Now, she could clearly remember how many hours her father had closeted himself in his hotel room, reading book after book that he brought with him from the mainland library. He'd been researching even then. She was sure he'd continued that research in the following summers when she had refused to go back. Refused to go back, Kate remembered, because of Ky Silver.

Ky had asked her to believe in fairy tales. He asked her to give him the impossible. When she refused, frightened, he shrugged and walked away without a second look. She had never gone back to the white sand and gulls since then.

Kate looked down again at her father's papers. She had to go back now—go back and finish what her father had started. Perhaps, more than the house, the trust fund, the antique jewelry that had been her mother's, this was her father's legacy to her. If she filed those papers neatly away, they'd haunt her for the rest of her life.

She had to go back, Kate reaffirmed as she took off her glasses and folded them neatly on the blotter. And it was Ky Silver she'd have to go to. Her father's aspirations had drawn her away from Ky once; now, four years later, they were drawing her back.

But Dr. Kathleen Hardesty knew the difference between fairy tales and reality. Reaching in her father's desk drawer, she drew out a sheet of thick creamy stationery and began to write.

Ky let the wind buffet him as he opened the throttle. He liked speed in much the same way he liked a lazy afternoon in the hammock. They were two of the things that made life worthwhile. He was used to the smell of salt spray, but he still inhaled deeply. He was well accustomed to the vibration of the deck under his feet, but he still felt it. He wasn't a man to let anything go unnoticed or unappreciated.

He grew up in this quiet, remote little coastal town, and though he'd traveled and intended to travel more, he didn't plan to live anywhere else. It suited him—the freedom of the sea, and the coziness of a small community.

He didn't resent the tourists because he knew they helped keep the village alive, but he preferred the island in winter. Then the storms blew wild and cold, and only the hearty would brave the ferry across Hatteras Inlet.

He fished, but unlike the majority of his neighbors, he rarely sold what he caught. What he pulled out of the sea, he ate. He dove, occasionally collecting shells, but again, this was for his own pleasure. Often he took tourists out on his boat to fish or to scuba dive, because there were times he enjoyed the company. But there were afternoons, like this sparkling one, when he simply wanted the sea to himself.

He had always been restless. His mother had said that he came into the world two weeks early because he grew impatient waiting. Ky turned thirty-two that spring, but was far from settled. He knew what he wanted—to live as he chose. The trouble was that he wasn't certain just what he wanted to choose.

At the moment, he chose the open sky and the endless sea. There were other moments when he knew that that wouldn't be enough.

But the sun was hot, the breeze cool and the shoreline was drawing near. The boat's motor was purring smoothly and in the small cooler was a tidy catch of fish he'd cook up for his supper that night. On a crystal, sparkling afternoon, perhaps it was enough.

From the shore he looked like a pirate might if there were pirates in the twentieth century. His hair was long enough to curl over his ears and well over the collar of a shirt had he worn one. It was black, a rich, true black that might have come from his Arapaho or Sicilian blood. His eyes were the deep, dark green of the sea on a cloudy day. His skin was bronzed from years in the sun, taut from the years of swimming and pulling in nets. His bone structure was also part of his heritage, sculpted, hard, defined.

When he smiled as he did now, racing the wind to shore, his face took on that reckless freedom women found irresistible. When he didn't smile, his eyes could turn as cold as a lion's before a leap. He discovered long ago that women found that equally irresistible.

Ky drew back on the throttle so that the boat slowed, rocked, then glided into its slip in Silver Lake Harbor.

With the quick, efficient movements of one born to the sea, he leaped onto the dock to secure the lines.

"Catch anything?"

Ky straightened and turned. He smiled, but absently, as one does at a brother seen almost every day of one's life. "Enough. Things slow at the Roost?"

Marsh smiled, and there was a brief flicker of family resemblance, but his eyes were a calm light brown and his hair was carefully styled. "Worried about your investment?"

Ky gave a half-shrug. "With you running things?"

Marsh didn't comment. They knew each other as intimately as men ever know each other. One was restless, the other calm. The opposition never seemed to matter. "Linda wants you to come up for dinner. She worries about you."

She would, Ky thought, amused. His sister-in-law loved to mother and fuss, even though she was five years younger than Ky. That was one of the reasons the restaurant she ran with Marsh was such a success—that, plus Marsh's business sense and the hefty investment and shrewd renovations Ky had made. Ky left the managing up to his brother and his sister-in-law. He didn't mind owning a restaurant, even keeping half an eye on the profit and loss, but he certainly had no interest in running one.

After the lines were secure, he wiped his palms down the hips of his cut-offs. "What's the special tonight?"

Marsh dipped his hands into his front pockets and rocked back on his heels. "Bluefish."

Grinning, Ky tossed back the lid of his cooler revealing his catch. "Tell Linda not to worry. I'll eat."

"That's not going to satisfy her." Marsh glanced at his brother as Ky looked out to sea. "She thinks you're alone too much."

"You're only alone too much if you don't like being alone." Ky glanced back over his shoulder. He didn't want to debate now, when the exhilaration of the speed and the sea were still upon him. But he'd never been a man to placate. "Maybe you two should think about having another baby, then Linda would be too busy to worry about big brothers."

"Give me a break. Hope's only eighteen months old."

"You've got to add nine to that," Ky reminded him carelessly. He was fond of his niece, despite—no, because she was a demon. "Anyway, it looks like the family lineage is in your hands."

"Yeah." Marsh shifted his feet, cleared his throat and fell silent. It was a habit he'd carried since childhood, one that could annoy or amuse Ky depending on his mood. At the moment, it was only mildly distracting.

Something was in the air. He could smell it, but he couldn't quite identify it. A storm brewing, he wondered? One of those hot, patient storms that seemed capable of brewing for weeks. He was certain he could smell it.

"Why don't you tell me what else is on your mind?" Ky suggested. "I want to get back to the house and clean these."

"You had a letter. It was put in our box by mistake."

It was a common enough occurrence, but by his brother's expression Ky knew there was more. His sense of an impending storm grew sharper. Saying nothing, he held out his hand.

"Ky..." Marsh began. There was nothing he could say, just as there'd been nothing to say four years before. Reaching in his back pocket, he drew out the letter.

The envelope was made from heavy cream-colored paper. Ky didn't have to look at the return address. The handwriting and the memories it brought leaped out at him. For a moment, he felt his breath catch in his lungs as it might if someone had caught him with a blow to the solar plexus. Deliberately, he expelled it. "Thanks," he said, as if it meant nothing. He stuck the letter in his pocket before he picked up his cooler and gear.

"Ky—" Again Marsh broke off. His brother had turned his head, and the cool, half-impatient stare said very clearly—back off. "If you change your mind about dinner," Marsh said.

"I'll let you know." Ky went down the length of the dock without looking back.

He was grateful he hadn't bothered to bring his car down to the harbor. He needed to walk. He needed the fresh air and the exercise to keep his mind clear while he remembered what he didn't want to remember. What he never really forgot.

Kate. Four years ago she'd walked out of his life with the same sort of cool precision with which she'd walked into it. She had reminded him of a Victorian doll—a little prim, a little aloof. He'd never had much patience with neatly folded hands or haughty manners, yet almost from the first instant he'd wanted her.

At first, he thought it was the fact that she was so different. A challenge—something for Ky Silver to conquer. He enjoyed teaching her to dive, and watching the precise step-by-step way she learned. It hadn't been any hardship to look at her in a snug scuba suit, although she didn't have voluptuous curves. She had a trim, neat, almost boylike figure and what seemed like yards of thick, soft hair.

He could still remember the first time she took it down from its pristine knot. It left him breathless, hurting, fascinated. Ky would have touched it—touched her then and there if her father hadn't been standing beside her. But if a man was clever, if a man was determined, he could find a way to be alone with a woman.

Ky had found ways. Kate had taken to diving as though she'd been born to it. While her father had buried himself in his books, Ky had taken Kate out on the water— under the water, to the silent, dreamlike world that had attracted her just as it had always attracted him.

He could remember the first time he kissed her. They had been wet and cool from a dive, standing on the deck of his boat. He was able to see the lighthouse behind her and the vague line of the coast. Her hair had flowed down her back, sleek from the water, dripping with it. He'd reached out and gathered it in his hand.

"What are you doing?"

Four years later, he could hear that low, cultured, eastern voice, the curiosity in it. It took no effort for him to see the curiosity that had been in her eyes.

"I'm going to kiss you."

The curiosity had remained in her eyes, fascinating him. "Why?"

"Because I want to."

It was as simple as that for him. He wanted to. Her body had stiffened as he'd drawn her against him. When her lips parted in protest, he closed his over them. In the time it takes a heart to beat, the rigidity had melted from her body. She'd kissed him with all the young, stored-up passion that had been in her—passion mixed with innocence. He was experienced enough to recognize her innocence, and that too had fascinated him. Ky had, foolishly, youthfully and completely, fallen in love.

Kate had remained an enigma to him, though they shared impassioned hours of laughter and long, lazy talks. He admired her thirst for learning and she had a predilection for putting knowledge into neat slots that baffled him. She was enthusiastic about diving, but it hadn't been enough for her simply to be able to swim freely underwater, taking her air from tanks. She had to know how the tanks worked, why they were fashioned a certain way. Ky watched her absorb what he told her, and knew she'd retain it.

They had taken walks along the shoreline at night and she had recited poetry from memory. Beautiful words, Byron, Shelley, Keats. And he, who'd never been overly impressed by such things, had eaten it up because her voice had made the words somehow personal. Then she'd begin to talk about syntax, iambic pentameters, and Ky would find new ways to divert her.

For three months, he did little but think of her. For the first time, Ky had considered changing his lifestyle. His little cottage near the beach needed work. It needed furniture. Kate would need more than milk crates and the hammock that had been his style. Because he'd been young and had never been in love before, Ky had taken his own plans for granted.

She'd walked out on him. She'd had her own plans, and he hadn't been part of them.

Her father came back to the island the following summer, and every summer thereafter. Kate never came back. Ky knew she had completed her doctorate and was teaching in a prestigious ivy league school where her father was all but a cornerstone. She had what she wanted. So, he told himself as he swung open the screen door of his cottage, did he. He went where he wanted, when he wanted. He called his own shots. His responsibilities extended only as far as he chose to extend them. To his way of thinking, that itself was a mark of success.

Setting the cooler on the kitchen floor, Ky opened the refrigerator. He twisted the top off a beer and drank half of it in one icy cold swallow. It washed some of the bitterness out of his mouth.

Calm now, and curious, he pulled the letter out of his pocket. Ripping it open, he drew out the single neatly written sheet.

Dear Ky,

You may or may not be aware that my father suffered a fatal heart attack two weeks ago. It was very sudden, and I'm currently trying to tie up the many details this involves.

In going through my father's papers, I find that he had again made arrangements to come to the island this summer, and engage your services. I now find it necessary to take his place. For reasons which I'd rather explain in person, I need your help. You have my father's deposit. When I arrive in Ocracoke on the fifteenth, we can discuss terms.

If possible, contact me at the hotel, or leave a message. I hope we'll be able to come to a mutually agreeable arrangement. Please give my best to Marsh. Perhaps I'll see him during my stay.

Best,
Kathleen Hardesty

So the old man was dead. Ky set down the letter and lifted his beer again. He couldn't say he'd had any liking for Edwin Hardesty. Kate's father had been a stringent,

humorless man. Still, he hadn't disliked him. Ky had, in
an odd way, gotten used to his company over the last few
summers. But this summer, it would be Kate.

Ky glanced at the letter again, then jogged his memory until he remembered the date. Two days, he mused.
She'd be there in two days...to discuss terms. A smile
played around the corners of his mouth but it didn't have
anything to do with humor. They'd discuss terms, he
agreed silently as he scanned Kate's letter again.

She wanted to take her father's place. Ky wondered if
she'd realized, when she wrote that, just how ironic it
was. Kathleen Hardesty had been obediently dogging her
father's footsteps all her life. Why should that change
after his death?

Had she changed? Ky wondered briefly. Would that
fascinating aura of innocence and aloofness still cling to
her? Or perhaps that had faded with the years. Would
that rather sweet primness have developed into a rigidity? He'd see for himself in a couple of days he realized,
but tossed the letter onto the counter rather than into the
trash.

So, she wanted to engage his services, he mused.
Leaning both hands on either side of the sink, he looked
out the window in the direction of the water he could
smell, but not quite see. She wanted a business arrangement—the rental of his boat, his gear and his time. He
felt the bitterness well up and swallowed it as cleanly as
he had the beer. She'd have her business arrangement.
And she'd pay. He'd see to that.

Ky left the kitchen with his catch still in the cooler. The
appetite he'd worked up with salt spray and speed had
vanished.

Kate pulled her car onto the ferry to Ocracoke and set
the brake. The morning was cool and very clear. Even so,

she was tempted to simply lean her head back and close her eyes. She wasn't certain what impulse had pushed her to drive from Connecticut rather than fly, but now that she'd all but reached her destination, she was too weary to analyze.

In the bucket seat beside her was her briefcase, and inside, all the papers she'd collected from her father's desk. Perhaps once she was in the hotel on the island, she could go through them again, understand them better. Perhaps the feeling that she was doing the right thing would come back. Over the last few days she'd lost that sense.

The closer she came to the island, the more she began to think she was making a mistake. Not to the island, Kate corrected ruthlessly—the closer she came to Ky. It was a fact, and Kate knew it was imperative to face facts so that they could be dealt with logically.

She had a little time left, a little time to calm the feelings that had somehow gotten stirred up during the drive south. It was foolish, and somehow it helped Kate to remind herself of that. She wasn't a woman returning to a lover, but a woman hoping to engage a diver in a very specific venture. Past personal feelings wouldn't enter into it because they were just that. Past.

The Kate Hardesty who'd arrived on Ocracoke four years ago had little to do with the Doctor Kathleen Hardesty who was going there now. She wasn't young, inexperienced or impressionable. Those reckless, wild traits of Ky's wouldn't appeal to her now. They wouldn't frighten her. They would be, if Ky agreed to her terms, business partners.

Kate felt the ferry move beneath her as she stared through the windshield. Yes, she thought, unless Ky had changed a great deal, the prospect of diving for treasure would appeal to his sense of adventure.

She knew enough about diving in the technical sense to be sure she'd find no one better equipped for the job. It was always advisable to have the best. More relaxed and less weary, Kate stepped out of her car to stand at the rail. From there she could watch the gulls swoop and the tiny uninhabited islands pass by. She felt a sense of homecoming, but pushed it away. Connecticut was home. Once Kate did what she came for, she'd go back.

The water swirled behind the boat. She couldn't hear it over the motor, but looking down she could watch the wake. One island was nearly imperceptible under a flock of big, brown pelicans. It made her smile, pleased to see the odd, awkward-looking birds again. They passed the long spit of land, where fishermen parked trucks and tried their luck, near the point where bay met sea. She could watch the waves crash and foam where there was no shore, just a turbulent marriage of waters. That was something she hadn't forgotten, though she hadn't seen it since she left the island. Nor had she forgotten just how treacherous the current was along that verge.

Excitement. She breathed deeply before she turned back to her car. The treacherous was always exciting.

When the ferry docked, she had only a short wait before she could drive her car onto the narrow blacktop. The trip to town wouldn't take long, and it wasn't possible to lose your way if you stayed on the one long road. The sea battered on one side, the sound flowed smoothly on the other—both were deep blue in the late morning light.

Her nerves were gone, at least that's what she told herself. It had just been a case of last minute jitters—very normal. She was prepared to see Ky again, speak to him, work with him if they could agree on the terms.

With the windows down, the soft moist air blew around her. It was soothing. She'd almost forgotten just how soothing air could be, or the sound of water lapping constantly against sand. It was right to come. When she saw the first faded buildings of the village, she felt a wave of relief. She was here. There was no turning back now.

The hotel where she had stayed that summer with her father was on the sound side of the island. It was small and quiet. If the service was a bit slow by northern standards, the view made up for it.

Kate pulled up in front and turned off the ignition. Self-satisfaction made her sigh. She'd taken the first step and was completely prepared for the next.

Then as she stepped out of the car, she saw him. For an instant, the confident professor of English literature vanished. She was only a woman, vulnerable to her own emotions.

Oh God, he hasn't changed. Not at all. As Ky came closer, she could remember every kiss, every murmur, every crazed storm of their loving. The breeze blew his hair back from his face so that every familiar angle and plane was clear to her. With the sun warm on her skin, bright in her eyes, she felt the years spin back, then forward again. He hadn't changed.

He hadn't expected to see her yet. Somehow he thought she'd arrive that afternoon. Yet he found it necessary to go by the Roost that morning knowing the restaurant was directly across from the hotel where she'd be staying.

She was here, looking neat and a bit too thin in her tailored slacks and blouse. Her hair was pinned up so that the soft femininity of her neck and throat were revealed. Her eyes seemed too dark against her pale skin—skin Ky knew would turn golden slowly under the summer sun.

She looked the same. Soft, prim, calm. Lovely. He ignored the thud in the pit of his stomach as he stepped in front of her. He looked her up and down with the arrogance that was so much a part of him. Then he grinned because he had an overwhelming urge to strangle her.

"Kate. Looks like my timing's good."

She was almost certain she couldn't speak and was therefore determined to speak calmly. "Ky, it's nice to see you again."

"Is it?"

Ignoring the sarcasm, Kate walked around to her trunk and released it. "I'd like to get together with you as soon as possible. There are some things I want to show you, and some business I'd like to discuss."

"Sure, always open for business."

He watched her pull two cases from her trunk, but didn't offer to help. He saw there was no ring on her hand—but it wouldn't have mattered.

"Perhaps we can meet this afternoon then, after I've settled in." The sooner the better, she told herself. They would establish the purpose, the ground rules and the payment. "We could have lunch in the hotel."

"No, thanks," he said easily, leaning against the side of her car while she set her cases down. "You want me, you know where to find me. It's a small island."

With his hands in the pockets of his jeans, he walked away from her. Though she didn't want to, Kate remembered that the last time he'd walked away, they'd stood in almost the same spot.

Picking up her cases, she headed for the hotel, perhaps a bit too quickly.

# Chapter Two

She knew where to find him. If the island had been double in size, she'd still have known where to find him. Kate acknowledged that Ky hadn't changed. That meant if he wasn't out on his boat, he would be at home, in the small, slightly dilapidated cottage he owned near the beach. Because she felt it would be a strategic error to go after him too soon, she dawdled over her unpacking.

But there were memories even here, where she'd spent one giddy, whirlwind night of love with Ky. It had been the only time they were able to sleep together through the night, embracing each other in the crisp hotel sheets until the first light of dawn crept around the edges of the window shades. She remembered how reckless she'd felt during those few stolen hours, and how dull the morning had seemed because it brought them to an end.

Now she could look out the same window she had stood by then, staring out in the same direction she'd stared out then when she watched Ky walk away. She remembered the sky had been streaked with a rose color before it had brightened to a pure, pale blue.

Then, with her skin still warm from her lover's touch and her mind glazed with lack of sleep and passion, Kate had believed such things could go on forever. But of course they couldn't. She had seen that only weeks later. Passion and reckless nights of loving had to give way to responsibilities, obligations.

Staring out the same window, in the same direction, Kate could feel the sense of loss she'd felt that long ago dawn without the underlying hope that they'd be together again. And again.

They wouldn't be together again, and there'd been no one else since that one heady summer. She had her career, her vocation, her books. She had had her taste of passion.

Turning away, she busied herself by rearranging everything she'd just arranged in her drawers and closet. When she decided she'd stalled in her hotel room long enough, Kate started out. She didn't take her car. She walked, just as she always walked to Ky's home.

She told herself she was over the shock of seeing him again. It was only natural that there be some strain, some discomfort. She was honest enough to admit that it would have been easier if there'd been only strain and discomfort, and not that one sharp quiver of pleasure. Kate acknowledged it, now that it had passed.

No, Ky Silver hadn't changed, she reminded herself. He was still arrogant, self-absorbed and cocky. Those traits might have appealed to her once, but she'd been very young. If she were wise, she could use those same traits to persuade Ky to help her. Yes, those traits, she thought, and the tempting offer of a treasure hunt. Even at her most pessimistic, she couldn't believe Ky would refuse. It was his nature to take chances.

This time she'd be in charge. Kate drew in a deep breath of warm air that tasted of sea. Somehow she felt it would steady her. Ky was going to find she was no longer naive, or susceptible to a few careless words of affection.

With her briefcase in hand, Kate walked through the village. This too was the same, she thought. She was glad of it. The simplicity and solitude still appealed to her. She enjoyed the dozens of little shops, the restaurants and small inns tucked here and there, all somehow using the harbor as a central point, the lighthouse as a landmark. The villagers still made the most of their notorious one-time resident and permanent ghost, Blackbeard. His name or face was lavishly displayed on store signs.

She passed the harbor, unconsciously scanning for Ky's boat. It was there, in the same slip he'd always used—clean lines, scrubbed deck, shining hardware. The flying bridge gleamed in the afternoon light and looked the same as she remembered. Reckless, challenging. The paint was fresh and there was no film of salt spray on the bridge windows. However careless Ky had been about his own appearance or his home, he'd always pampered his boat.

The *Vortex*. Kate studied the flamboyant lettering on the stern. He could pamper, she thought again, but he also expected a lot in return. She knew the speed he could urge out of the second-hand cabin cruiser he'd lovingly reconstructed himself. Nothing could block the image of the days she'd stood beside him at the helm. The wind had whipped her hair as he'd laughed and pushed for speed, and more speed. Her heart thudded, her pulse raced until she was certain nothing and no one could catch them. She'd been afraid, of him, of the rush of wind—but she'd stayed with both. In the end, she'd left both.

He enjoyed the demanding, the thrilling, the frightening. Kate gripped the handle of her briefcase tighter. Isn't that why she came to him? There were dozens of other experienced divers, many, many other experts on the coastal waters of the Outer Banks. There was only one Ky Silver.

"Kate? Kate Hardesty?"

At the sound of her name, Kate turned and felt the years tumble back again. "Linda!" This time there was no restraint. With an openness she showed to very few, Kate embraced the woman who dashed up to her, "It's wonderful to see you." With a laugh, she drew Linda away to study her. The same chestnut hair cut short and pert, the same frank, brown eyes. It seemed very little had changed on the island. "You look wonderful."

"When I looked out the window and saw you, I could hardly believe it. Kate, you've barely changed at all." With her usual candor and lack of pretention, Linda took a quick, thorough survey. It was quick only because she did things quickly, but it wasn't subtle. "You're too thin," she decided. "But that might be jealousy."

"You still look like a college freshman," Kate returned. "That is jealousy."

As swiftly as the laugh had come, Linda sobered. "I'm sorry about your father, Kate. These past weeks must've been difficult for you."

Kate heard the sincerity, but she'd already tied up her grief and stored it away. "Ky told you?"

"Ky never tells me anything," Linda said with a sniff. In an unconscious move, she glanced in the direction of his boat. It was in its slip and Kate had been walking north—in the direction of Ky's cottage. There could be only one place she could have been going. "Marsh did. How long are you going to stay?"

"I'm not sure yet." She felt the weight of her briefcase. Dreams held the same weight as responsibilities. "There are some things I have to do."

"One of the things you have to do is have dinner at the Roost tonight. It's the restaurant right across from your hotel."

Kate looked back at the rough wooden sign. "Yes, I noticed it. Is it new?"

Linda glanced over her shoulder with a self-satisfied nod. "By Ocracoke standards. We run it."

"We?"

"Marsh and I." With a beaming smile, Linda held out her left hand. "We've been married for three years." Then she rolled her eyes in a habit Kate remembered. "It only took me fifteen years to convince him he couldn't live without me."

"I'm happy for you." She was, and if she felt a pang, she ignored it. "Married and running a restaurant. My father never filled me in on island gossip."

"We have a daughter too. Hope. She's a year and a half old and a terror. For some reason, she takes after Ky." Linda sobered again, laying a hand lightly on Kate's arm. "You're going to see him now." It wasn't a question; she didn't bother to disguise it as one.

"Yes." Keep it casual, Kate ordered herself. Don't let the questions and concern in Linda's eyes weaken you. There were ties between Linda and Ky, not only newly formed family ones, but the older tie of the island. "My father was working on something. I need Ky's help with it."

Linda studied Kate's calm face. "You know what you're doing?"

"Yes." She didn't show a flicker of unease. Her stomach slowly wrapped itself in knots. "I know what I'm doing."

"Okay." Accepting Kate's answer, but not satisfied, Linda dropped her hand. "Please come by—the restaurant or the house. We live just down the road from Ky. Marsh'll want to see you, and I'd like to show off Hope—

and our menu," she added with a grin. "Both are out-standing."

"Of course I'll come by." On impulse, she took both of Linda's hands. "It's really good to see you again. I know I didn't keep in touch, but—"

"I understand." Linda gave her hands a quick squeeze. "That was yesterday. I've got to get back, the lunch crowd's pretty heavy during the season." She let out a little sigh, wondering if Kate was as calm as she seemed. And if Ky were as big a fool as ever. "Good luck," she murmured, then dashed across the street again.

"Thanks," Kate said under her breath. She was going to need it.

The walk was as beautiful as she remembered. She passed the little shops with their display windows showing hand-made crafts or antiques. She passed the blue and white clapboard houses and the neat little streets on the outskirts of town with their bleached green lawns and leafy trees.

A dog raced back and forth on the length of his chain as she wandered by, barking at her as if he knew he was supposed to but didn't have much interest in it. She could see the tower of the white lighthouse. There'd been a keeper there once, but those days were over. Then she was on the narrow path that led to Ky's cottage.

Her palms were damp. She cursed herself. If she had to remember, she'd remember later, when she was alone. When she was safe.

The path was as it had been, just wide enough for a car, sparsely graveled, lined with bushes that always grew out a bit too far. The bushes and trees had always had a wild, overgrown look that suited the spot. That suited him.

Ky had told her he didn't care much for visitors. If he wanted company, all he had to do was go into town where he knew everyone. That was typical of Ky Silver, Kate mused. If I want you, I'll let you know. Otherwise, back off.

He'd wanted her once.... Nervous, Kate shifted the briefcase to her other hand. Whatever he wanted now, he'd have to hear her out. She needed him for what he was best at—diving and taking chances.

When the house came into view, she stopped, staring. It was still small, still primitive. But it no longer looked as though it would keel over on its side in a brisk wind.

The roof had been redone. Obviously Ky wouldn't need to set out pots and pans during a rain any longer. The porch he'd once talked vaguely about building now ran the length of the front, sturdy and wide. The screen door that had once been patched in a half a dozen places had been replaced by a new one. Yet nothing looked new, she observed. It just looked right. The cedar had weathered to silver, the windows were untrimmed but gleaming. There was, much to her surprise, a spill of impatiens in a long wooden planter.

She'd been wrong, Kate decided as she walked closer. Ky Silver had changed. Precisely how, and precisely how much, she had yet to find out.

She was nearly to the first step when she heard sounds coming from the rear of the house. There was a shed back there, she remembered, full of boards and tools and salvage. Grateful that she didn't have to meet him in the house, Kate walked around the side to the tiny backyard. She could hear the sea and knew it was less than a two-minute walk through high grass and sand dunes.

Did he still go down there in the evenings? she wondered. Just to look, he'd said. Just to smell. Sometimes he'd pick up driftwood or shells or whatever small treasures the sea gave up to the sand. Once he'd given her a small smooth shell that fit into the palm of her hand—very white with a delicate pink center. A woman with her first gift of diamonds could not have been more thrilled.

Shaking the memories away, she went into the shed. It was as tall as the cottage and half as wide. The last time she'd been there, it'd been crowded with planks and boards and boxes of hardware. Now she saw the hull of a boat. At a work table with his back to her, Ky sanded the mast.

"You've built it." The words came out before she could stop them, full of astonished pleasure. How many times had he told her about the boat he'd build one day? It had seemed to Kate it had been his only concrete ambition. Mahogany on oak, he'd said. A seventeen-foot sloop that would cut through the water like a dream. He'd have bronze fastenings and teak on the deck. One day he'd sail the inner coastal waters from Ocracoke to New England. He'd described the boat so minutely that she'd seen it then just as clearly as she saw it now.

"I told you I would." Ky turned away from the mast and faced her. She, in the doorway, had the sun at her back. He was half in shadow.

"Yes." Feeling foolish, Kate tightened her grip on the briefcase. "You did."

"But you didn't believe me." Ky tossed aside the sandpaper. Did she have to look so neat and cool, and impossibly lovely? A trickle of sweat ran down his back. "You always had a problem seeing beyond the moment."

Reckless, impatient, compelling. Would he always bring those words to her mind? "You always had a problem dealing with the moment," she said.

His brow lifted, whether in surprise or derision she couldn't be sure. "Then it might be said *we* always had a problem." He walked to her, so that the sun slanting through the small windows fell over him, then behind him. "But it didn't always seem to matter." To satisfy himself that he still could, Ky reached out and touched her face. She didn't move, and her skin was as soft and cool as he remembered. "You look tired Kate."

The muscles in her stomach quivered, but not her voice. "It was a long trip."

His thumb brushed along her cheekbone. "You need some sun."

This time she backed away. "I intend to get some."

"So I gathered from your letter." Pleased that she'd retreated first, Ky leaned against the open door. "You wrote that you wanted to talk to me in person. You're here. Why don't you tell me what you want?"

The cocky grin might have made her melt once. Now it stiffened her spine. "My father was researching a project. I intend to finish it."

"So?"

"I need your help."

Ky laughed and stepped past her into the sunlight. He needed the air, the distance. He needed to touch her again. "From your tone, there's nothing you hate more than asking me for it."

"No." She stood firm, feeling suddenly strong and bitter. "Nothing."

There was no humor in his eyes as he faced her again. The expression in them was cold and flat. She'd seen it before. "Then let's understand each other before we start. You left the island and me, and took what I wanted."

He couldn't make her cringe now as he once had with only that look. "What happened four years ago has nothing to do with today."

"The hell it doesn't." He came toward her again so that she took an involuntary step backward. "Still afraid of me?" he asked softly.

As it had a moment ago, the question turned the fear to anger. "No," she told him, and meant it. "I'm not afraid of you, Ky. I've no intention of discussing the past, but I will agree that I left the island and you. I'm here now on business. I'd like you to hear me out. If you're interested, we'll discuss terms, nothing else."

"I'm not one of your students, professor." The drawl crept into his voice, as it did when he let it. "Don't instruct."

She curled her fingers tighter around the handle of her briefcase. "In business, there are always ground rules."

"Nobody agreed to let you make them."

"I made a mistake," Kate said quietly as she fought for control. "I'll find someone else."

She'd taken only two steps away when Ky grabbed her arm. "No, you won't." The stormy look in his eyes made her throat dry. She knew what he meant. She'd never find anyone else that could make her feel as he made her feel, or want as he made her want. Deliberately, Kate removed his hand from her arm.

"I came here on business. I've no intention of fighting with you over something that doesn't exist any longer."

"We'll see about that." How long could he hold on? Ky wondered. It hurt just to look at her and to feel her withdrawing with every second that went by. "But for now, why don't you tell me what you have in that businesslike briefcase, professor."

Kate took a deep breath. She should have known it wouldn't be easy. Nothing was ever easy with Ky. "Charts," she said precisely. "Notebooks full of research, maps, carefully documented facts and precise theories. In my opinion, my father was very close to pinpointing the exact location of the *Liberty*, an English merchant vessel that sank, stores intact, off the North Carolina coast two hundred and fifty years ago."

He listened without a comment or a change of expression from beginning to end. When she finished, Ky studied her face for one long moment. "Come inside," he said and turned toward the house. "Show me what you've got."

His arrogance made her want to turn away and go back to town exactly as she'd come. There were other divers, others who knew the coast and the waters as well as Ky did. Kate forced herself to calm down, forced herself to think. There were others, but if it was a choice between the devil she knew and the unknown, she had no choice. Kate followed him into the house.

This, too, had changed. The kitchen she remembered had had a paint splattered floor, with the only usable counter space being a tottering picnic table. The floor had been stripped and varnished, the cabinets redone, and scrubbed butcher block counters lined the sink. He had put in a skylight so that the sun spilled down over the picnic table, now re-worked and re-painted, with benches along either side.

"Did you do all of this yourself?"

"Yeah. Surprised?"

So he didn't want to make polite conversation. Kate set her briefcase on the table. "Yes. You always seemed content that the walls were about to cave in on you."

"I was content with a lot of things, once. Want a beer?"

"No." Kate sat down and drew the first of her father's notebooks out of her briefcase. "You'll want to read these. It would be unnecessary and time-consuming for you to read every page, but if you'd look over the ones I've marked, I think you'll have enough to go by."

"All right." Ky turned from the refrigerator, beer in hand. He sat, watching her over the rim as he took the first swallow, then he opened the notebook.

Edwin Hardesty's handwriting was very clear and precise. He wrote down his facts in didactic, unromantic terms. What could have been exciting was as dry as a thesis, but it was accurate. Ky had no doubt of that.

The *Liberty* had been lost, with its stores of sugar, tea, silks, wine and other imports for the colonies. Hardesty had listed the manifest down to the last piece of hardtack. When it had left England, the ship had also been carrying gold. Twenty-five thousand in coins of the realm. Ky glanced up from the notebook to see Kate watching him.

"Interesting," he said simply, and turned to the next page she marked.

There'd been only three survivors who'd washed up on the island. One of the crew had described the storm that had sunk the *Liberty*, giving details on the height of the waves, the splintering wood, the water gushing into the hole. It was a grim, grisly story which Hardesty had recounted in his pragmatic style, complete with footnotes. The crewman had also given the last known location of the ship before it had gone down. Ky didn't require Hardesty's calculations to figure the ship had sunk two-and-a-half miles off the coast of Ocracoke.

Going from one notebook to another, Ky read through Hardesty's well drafted theories, his clear to-the-point documentations, corroborated and recorroborated. He scanned the charts, then studied them with more care. He remembered the man's avid interest in diving, which had always seemed inconsistent with his precise life-style.

So he'd been looking for gold, Ky mused. All these years the man had been digging in books and looking for gold. If it had been anyone else, Ky might have dismissed it as another fable. Little towns along the coast were full of stories about buried treasure. Edward Teach had used the shallow waters of the inlets to frustrate and outwit the crown until his last battle off the shores of Ocracoke. That alone kept the dreams of finding sunken treasures alive.

But it was Doctor Edwin J. Hardesty, Yale professor, an unimaginative, humorless man who didn't believe there was time to be wasted on the frivolous, who'd written these notebooks.

Ky might still have dismissed it, but Kate was sitting across from him. He had enough adventurous blood in him to believe in destinies.

Setting the last notebook aside, he picked up his beer again. "So, you want to treasure hunt."

She ignored the humor in his voice. With her hands folded on the table, she leaned forward. "I intend to follow through with what my father was working on."

"Do you believe it?"

Did she? Kate opened her mouth and closed it again. She had no idea. "I don't believe that all of my father's time and research should go for nothing. I want to try. As it happens, I need you to help me do it. You'll be compensated."

"Will I?" He studied the liquid left in the beer bottle with a half smile. "Will I indeed?"

"I need you, your boat and your equipment for a month, maybe two. I can't dive alone because I just don't know the waters well enough to risk it, and I don't have the time to waste. I have to be back in Connecticut by the end of August."

"To get more chalk dust under your fingernails."

She sat back slowly. "You have no right to criticize my profession."

"I'm sure the chalk's very exclusive at Yale," Ky commented. "So you're giving yourself six weeks or so to find a pot of gold."

"If my father's calculations·are viable, it won't take that long."

"If," Ky repeated. Setting down his bottle, he leaned forward. "I've got no timetable. You want six weeks of my time, you can have it. For a price."

"Which is?"

"A hundred dollars a day and fifty percent of whatever we find."

Kate gave him a cool look as she slipped the notebooks back into her briefcase. "Whatever I was four years ago, Ky, I'm not a fool now. A hundred dollars a day is outrageous when we're dealing with monthly rates. And fifty percent is out of the question." It gave her a certain satisfaction to bargain with him. This made it business, pure and simple. "I'll give you fifty dollars a day and ten percent."

With the maddening half grin on his face he swirled the beer in the bottle. "I don't turn my boat on for fifty a day."

She tilted her head a bit to study him. Something tore inside him. She'd often done that whenever he said something she wanted to think over. "You're more mercenary than you once were."

"We've all got to make a living, professor." Didn't she feel anything? he thought furiously. Wasn't she suffering just a little, being in the house where they'd made love their first and last time? "You want a service," he said quietly, "you pay for it. Nothing's free. Seventy-five a day and twenty-five percent. We'll say it's for old-times' sake."

"No, we'll say it's for business sake." She made herself extend her hand, but when his closed over it, she regretted the gesture. It was calloused, hard, strong. Kate knew how his hand felt skimming over her skin, driving her to desperation, soothing, teasing, seducing.

"We have a deal." Ky thought he could see a flash of remembrance in her eyes. He kept her hand in his knowing she didn't welcome his touch. Because she didn't. "There's no guarantee you'll find your treasure."

"That's understood."

"Fine. I'll deduct your father's deposit from the total."

"All right." With her free hand, she clutched at her briefcase. "When do we start?"

"Meet me at the harbor at eight tomorrow." Deliberately, he placed his other free hand over hers on the leather case. "Leave this with me. I want to look over the papers some more."

"There's no need for you to have them," Kate began, but his hands tightened on hers.

"If you don't trust me with them, you take them along." His voice was very smooth and very quiet. At its most dangerous. "And find yourself another diver."

Their gazes locked. Her hands were trapped and so was she. Kate knew there would be sacrifices she'd have to make. "I'll meet you at eight."

"Fine." He released her hands and sat back. "Nice doing business with you, Kate."

Dismissed, she rose. Just how much had she sacrificed already? she wondered. "Goodbye."

He lifted and drained his half-finished beer when the screen shut behind her. Then he made himself sit there until he was certain that when he rose and walked to the window she'd be out of sight. He made himself sit there until the air flowing through the screens had carried her scent away.

Sunken ships and deep-sea treasure. It would have excited him, captured his imagination, enthusiasm and interest if he hadn't had an overwhelming urge to just get in his boat and head toward the horizon. He hadn't believed she could still affect him that way, that much, that completely. He'd forgotten that just being within touching distance of her tied his stomach in knots.

He'd never gotten over her. No matter what he filled his life with over the past four years, he'd never gotten over the slim, intellectual woman with the haughty face and doe's eyes.

Ky sat, staring at the briefcase with her initials stamped discreetly near the handle. He'd never expected her to come back, but he'd just discovered he'd never accepted the fact that she'd left him. Somehow, he'd managed to deceive himself through the years. Now, seeing her again, he knew it had just been a matter of pure survival and nothing to do with truth. He'd had to go on, to pretend that that part of his life was behind him, or he would have gone mad.

She was back now, but she hadn't come back to him. A business arrangement. Ky ran his hand over the smooth leather of the case. She simply wanted the best diver she knew and was willing to pay for him. Fee for services, nothing more, nothing less. The past meant little or nothing to her.

Fury grew until his knuckles whitened around the bottle. He'd give her what she paid for, he promised himself. And maybe a bit extra.

This time when she went away, he wouldn't be left feeling like an inadequate fool. She'd be the one who would have to go on pretending for the rest of her life. This time when she went away, he'd be done with her. God, he'd have to be.

Rising quickly, he went out to the shed. If he stayed inside, he'd give in to the need to get very, very drunk.

# Chapter Three

Kate had the water in the tub so hot that the mirror over the white pedestal sink was fogged. Oil floated on the surface, subtly fragrant and soothing. She'd lost track of how long she lay there—soaking, recharging. The next irrevocable step had been taken. She'd survived. Somehow during her discussion with Ky in his kitchen she had fought back the memories of laughter and passion. She couldn't count how many meals they'd shared there, cooking their catch, sipping wine.

Somehow during the walk back to her hotel, she'd overcome the need to weep. Tomorrow would be just a little easier. Tomorrow, and every day that followed. She had to believe it.

His animosity would help. His derision toward her kept Kate from romanticizing what she had to tell herself had never been more than a youthful summer fling. Perspective. She'd always been able to stand back and align everything in its proper perspective.

Perhaps her feelings for Ky weren't as dead as she had hoped or pretended they were. But her emotions were tinged with bitterness. Only a fool asked for more sorrow. Only a romantic believed that bitterness could ever be sweet. It had been a long time since Kate had been a romantic fool. Even so, they would work together because both had an interest in what might be lying on the sea floor.

Think of it. Two hundred and fifty years. Kate closed her eyes and let her mind drift. The silks and sugar would be gone, but would they find brass fittings deep in corrosion after two-and-a-half centuries? The hull would be covered with fungus and barnacles, but how much of the oak would still be intact? Might the log have been secured in a waterproof hold and still be legible? It could be donated to a museum in her father's name. It would be something—the last something she could do for him. Perhaps then she'd be able to lay all her ambiguous feelings to rest.

The gold, Kate thought as she rose from the tub, the gold would survive. She wasn't immune to the lure of it. Yet she knew it would be the hunt that would be exciting, and somehow fulfilling. If she found it...

What would she do? Kate wondered. She dropped the hotel towel over the rod before she wrapped herself in her robe. Behind her, the mirror was still fogged with steam from the water that drained slowly from the tub. Would she put her share tidily in some conservative investments? Would she take a leisurely trip to the Greek islands to see what Byron had seen and fallen in love with there? With a laugh, Kate walked through to the other room to pick up her brush. Strange, she hadn't thought beyond the search yet. Perhaps that was for the best, it wasn't wise to plan too far ahead.

*You always had a problem seeing beyond the moment.*

Damn him! With a sudden fury, Kate slammed the brush onto the dresser. She'd seen beyond the moment. She'd seen that he'd offered her no more than a tentative affair in a run-down beach shack. No guarantees, no commitment, no future. She only thanked God she'd had enough of her senses left to understand it and to walk away from what was essentially nothing at all. She'd never let Ky know just how horribly it had hurt to walk away from nothing at all.

Her father had been right to quietly point out the weaknesses in Ky, and her obligation to herself and her chosen profession. Ky's lack of ambition, his careless attitude toward the future weren't qualities, but flaws. She'd had a responsibility, and by accepting it had given herself independence and satisfaction.

Calmer, she picked up her brush again. She was dwelling on the past too much. It was time to stop. With the deft movements of habit, she secured her hair into a sleek twist. From this time on, she'd think only of what was to come, not what had, or might have been.

She needed to get out.

With panic just under the surface, Kate pulled a dress out of her closet. It no longer mattered that she was tired, that all she really wanted to do was to crawl into bed and let her mind and body rest. Nerves wouldn't permit it. She'd go across the street, have a drink with Linda and Marsh. She'd see their baby, have a long, extravagant dinner. When she came back to the hotel, alone, she'd make certain she'd be too tired for dreams.

Tomorrow, she had work to do.

Because she dressed quickly, Kate arrived at the Roost just past six. What she saw, she immediately approved of. It wasn't elegant, but it was comfortable. It didn't have the dimly lit, cathedral feel of so many of the restaurants she'd dined in with her father, with colleagues, back in Connecticut. It was relaxed, welcoming, cozy.

There were paintings of ships and boats along the stuccoed walls, of armadas and cutters. Throughout the dining room was other sailing paraphernalia—a ship's compass with its brass gleaming, a colorful spinnaker draped behind the bar with the stools in front of it shaped like wooden kegs. There was a crow's nest spearing toward the ceiling with ferns spilling out and down the mast.

The room was already half full of couples and families, the bulk of whom Kate identified as tourists. She could hear the comforting sound of cutlery scraping lightly over plates. There was the smell of good food and the hum of mixed conversations.

Comfortable, she thought again, but definitely well organized. Waiters and waitresses in sailor's denims moved smoothly, making every second count without looking rushed. The window opened out to a full evening view of Silver Lake Harbor. Kate turned her back on it because she knew her gaze would fall on the *Vortex* or its empty slip.

Tomorrow was soon enough for that. She wanted one night without memories.

"Kate."

She felt the hands on her shoulders and recognized the voice. There was a smile on her face when she turned around. "Marsh, I'm so glad to see you."

In his quiet way, he studied her, measured her and saw both the strain and the relief. In the same way, he'd had a crush on her that had faded into admiration and respect before the end of that one summer. "Beautiful as ever. Linda said you were, but it's nice to see for myself."

She laughed, because he'd always been able to make her feel as though life could be honed down to the most simple of terms. She'd never questioned why that trait had made her relax with Marsh and tingle with Ky.

"Several congratulations are in order, I hear. On your marriage, your daughter and your business."

"I'll take them all. How about the best table in the house?"

"No less than I expected." She linked her arm through his. "Your life agrees with you," she decided as he led her to a table by the window. "You look happy."

"Look and am." He lifted a hand to brush hers. "We were sorry to hear about your father, Kate."

"I know. Thank you."

Marsh sat across from her and fixed her with eyes so much calmer, so much softer than his brother's. She'd always wondered why the man with the dreamer's eyes had been so practical while Ky had been the real dreamer. "It's tragic, but I can't say I'm sorry it brought you back to the island. We've missed you." He paused, just long enough for effect. "All of us."

Kate picked up the square carmine-colored napkin and ran it through her hands. "Things change," she said deliberately. "You and Linda are certainly proof of that. When I left, you thought she was a bit of a nuisance."

"That hasn't changed," he claimed and grinned. He glanced up at the young, pony-tailed waitress. "This is Cindy, she'll take good care of you, Miss Hardesty—" He looked back at Kate with a grin. "I guess I should say Dr. Hardesty."

"Miss'll do," Kate told him. "I've taken the summer off."

"Miss Hardesty's a guest, a special one," he added, giving the waitress a smile. "How about a drink before you order? Or a bottle of wine?"

"Piesporter," the reply came from a deep, masculine voice.

Kate's fingers tightened on the linen, but she forced herself to look up calmly to meet Ky's amused eyes.

"The professor has a fondness for it."

"Yes, Mr. Silver."

Before Kate could agree or disagree, the waitress had dashed off.

"Well, Ky," Marsh commented easily. "You have a way of making the help come to attention."

With a shrug, Ky leaned against his brother's chair. If the three of them felt the air was suddenly tighter, each concealed it in their own way. "I had an urge for scampi."

"I can recommend it," Marsh told Kate. "Linda and the chef debated the recipe, then babied it until they reached perfection."

Kate smiled at Marsh as though there were no dark, brooding man looking down at her. "I'll try it. Are you going to join me?"

"I wish I could. Linda had to run home and deal with some crisis—Hope has a way of creating them and browbeating the babysitter—but I'll try to get back for coffee. Enjoy your dinner." Rising, he sent his brother a cool, knowing look, then walked away.

"Marsh never completely got over that first case of adulation," Ky commented, then took his brother's seat without invitation.

"Marsh has always been a good friend." Kate draped the napkin over her lap with great care. "Though I realize this is your brother's restaurant, Ky, I'm sure you don't want my company for dinner any more than I want yours."

"That's where you're wrong." He sent a quick, dashing smile at the waitress as she brought the wine. He didn't bother to correct Kate's assumption on the Roost's ownership. Kate sat stone-faced, her manners too good to allow her to argue, while Cindy opened the bottle and poured the first sip for Ky to taste.

"It's fine," he told her. "I'll pour." Taking the bottle, he filled Kate's glass to within half an inch of the rim. "Since we've both chosen the Roost tonight, why don't we have a little test?"

Kate lifted her glass and sipped. The wine was cool and dry. She remembered the first bottle they'd shared—sitting on the floor of his cottage the night she gave him her innocence. Deliberately, she took another swallow. "What kind of test?"

"We can see if the two of us can share a civilized meal in public. That was something we never got around to before."

Kate frowned as he lifted his glass. She'd never seen Ky drink from a wine glass. The few times they had indulged in wine, it had been drunk out of one of the half a dozen water glasses he'd owned. The stemware seemed too delicate for his hand, the wine too mellow for the look in his eye.

No, they'd never eaten dinner in public before. Her father would have exuded disapproval for socializing with someone he'd considered an employee. Kate had known it, and hadn't risked it.

Things were different now, she told herself as she lifted her own glass. In a sense, Ky was now her employee. She could make her own judgments. Recklessly, she toasted him. "To a profitable arrangement then."

"I couldn't have said it better myself." He touched the rim of his glass to hers, but his gaze was direct and uncomfortable. "Blue suits you," he said, referring to her dress, but not taking his eyes off hers. "The deep midnight blue that makes your skin look like something that should be tasted very, very carefully."

She stared at him, stunned at how easily his voice could take on that low, intimate tone that had always made the blood rush out of her brain. He'd always been able to make words seem something dark and secret. That had been one of his greatest skills, one she had never been prepared for. She was no more prepared for it now.

"Would you care to order now?" The waitress stopped beside the table, cheerful, eager to please.

Ky smiled when Kate remained silent. "We're having scampi. The house dressing on the salads will be fine." He leaned back, glass in hand, still smiling. But the smile on his lips didn't connect with his eyes. "You're not drinking your wine. Maybe I should've asked if your taste has changed over the years."

"It's fine." Deliberately she sipped, then kept the glass in her hand as though it would anchor her. "Marsh looks well," she commented. "I was happy to hear about him and Linda. I always pictured them together."

"Did you?" Ky lifted his glass toward the lowering evening light slanting through the window. He watched the colors spear through the wine and glass and onto Kate's hand. "He didn't. But then..." Shifting his gaze, he met her eyes again. "Marsh always took more time to make up his mind than me."

"Recklessness," she continued as she struggled just to breathe evenly, "was always more your style than your brother's."

"But you didn't come to my brother with your charts and notes, did you?"

"No." With an effort she kept her voice and her eyes level. "I didn't. Perhaps I decided a certain amount of recklessness had its uses."

"Find me useful, do you, Kate?"

The waitress served the salads but didn't speak this time. She saw the look in Ky's eyes.

So had Kate. "When I'm having a job done, I've found that it saves a considerable amount of time and trouble to find the most suitable person." With forced calm, she set down her wine and picked up her fork. "I wouldn't have come back to Ocracoke for any other reason." She tilted her head, surprised by the quick surge of challenge that rushed through her. "Things will be simpler for both of us if that's clear up front."

Anger moved through him, but he controlled it. If they were playing word games, he had to keep his wits. She'd always been clever, but now it appeared the cleverness was glossed over with sophistication. He remembered the innocent, curious Kate with a pang. "As I recall, you were always one for complicating rather than simplifying. I had to explain the purpose, history and mechanics of every piece of equipment before you'd take the first dive."

"That's called caution, not complication."

"You'd know more about caution than I would. Some people spend half their lives testing the wind." He drank deeply of wine. "I'd rather ride with it."

"Yes." This time it was she who smiled with her lips only. "I remember very well. No plans, no ties, tomorrow the wind might change."

"If you're anchored in one spot too long, you can become like those trees out there." He gestured out the window where a line of sparse junipers bent away from the sea. "Stunted."

"Yet you're still here, where you were born, where you grew up."

Slowly Ky poured her more wine. "The island's too isolated, the life a bit too basic for some. I prefer it to those structured little communities with their parties and country clubs."

Kate looked like she belonged in such a place, Ky thought as he fought against the frustrated desire that ebbed and flowed inside him. She belonged in an elegant silk suit, holding a Dresden cup and discussing an obscure eighteenth-century English poet. Was that why she could still make him feel rough and awkward and too full of longings?

If they could be swept back in time, he'd have stolen her, taken her out to open sea and kept her there. They would have traveled from port to exotic port. If having her meant he could never go home again, then he'd have sailed until his time was up. But he would have had her. Ky's fingers tightened around his glass. By God, he would have had her.

The main course was slipped in front of him discreetly. Ky brought himself back to the moment. It wasn't the eighteenth century, but today. Still, she had brought him the past with the papers and maps. Perhaps they'd both find more than they'd bargained for.

"I looked over the things you left with me."

"Oh?" She felt a quick tingle of excitement but speared the first delicate shrimp as though it were all that concerned her.

"Your father's research is very thorough."

"Of course."

Ky let out a quick laugh. "Of course," he repeated, toasting her. "In any case, I think he might have been on the right track. You do realize that the section he narrowed it down to goes into a dangerous area."

Her brows drew together, but she continued to eat. "Sharks?"

"Sharks are a little difficult to confine to an area," he said easily. "A lot of people forget that the war came this close in the forties. There are still mines all along the coast of the Outer Banks. If we're going down to the bottom, it'd be smart to keep that in mind.''

"I've no intention of being careless."

"No, but sometimes people look so far ahead they don't see what's under their feet."

Though he'd eaten barely half of his meal, Ky picked up his wine again. How could he eat when his whole system was aware of her? He couldn't stop himself from wondering what it would be like to pull those confining pins out of her hair as he'd done so often in the past. He couldn't prevent the memory from springing up about what it had been like to bundle her into his arms and just hold her there with her body fitting so neatly against his. He could picture those long, serious looks she'd give him just before passion would start to take over, then the freedom he could feel racing through her in those last heady moments of love-making.

How could it have been so right once and so wrong now? Wouldn't her body still fit against his? Wouldn't her hair flow through his hands as it fell—that quiet brown that took on such fascinating lights in the sun. She'd always murmur his name after passion was spent, as if the sound alone sustained her. He wanted to hear her say it, just once more, soft and breathless while they were tangled together, bodies still warm and pulsing. He wasn't sure he could resist it.

Absently Ky signaled for coffee. Perhaps he didn't want to resist it. He needed her. He'd forgotten just how sharp and sure a need could be. Perhaps he'd take her. He didn't believe she was indifferent to him—certain things never fade completely. In his own time, in his own way, he'd take what he once had from her. And pray it would be enough this time.

When he looked back at her, Kate felt the warning signals shiver through her. Ky was a difficult man to understand. She knew only that he'd come to some decision and that it involved her. Grateful for the warming effects of the coffee, she drank. She was in charge this time, she reminded herself, every step of the way and she'd make him aware of it. There was no time like the present to begin.

"I'll be at the harbor at eight," she said briskly. "I'll require tanks of course, but I brought my own wet suit. I'd appreciate it if you'd have my briefcase and its contents on board. I believe we'd be wise to spend between six and eight hours out a day."

"Have you kept up with your diving?"

"I know what to do."

"I'd be the last to argue that you had the best teacher." He tilted his cup back in a quick, impatient gesture Kate found typical of him. "But if you're rusty, we'll take it slow for a day or two."

"I'm a perfectly competent diver."

"I want more than competence in a partner."

He saw the flare in her eyes and his need sharpened. It was a rare and arousing thing to watch her controlled and reasonable temperament heat up. "We're not partners. You're working for me."

"A matter of viewpoint," Ky said easily. He rose, deliberately blocking her in. "We'll be putting in a full day tomorrow, so you'd better go catch up on all the sleep you've been missing lately."

"I don't need you to worry about my health, Ky."

"I worry about my own," he said curtly. "You don't go under with me unless you're rested and alert. You come to the harbor in the morning with shadows under your eyes, you won't make the first dive." Furiously she squashed the urge to argue with the reasonable. "If you're sluggish, you make mistakes," Ky said briefly. "A mistake you make can cost me. That logical enough for you, professor?"

"It's perfectly clear." Bracing herself for the brush of bodies, Kate rose. But bracing herself didn't stop the jolt, not for either of them.

"I'll walk you back."

"It's not necessary."

His hand curled over her wrist, strong and stubborn. "It's civilized," he said lazily. "You were always big on being civilized."

Until you'd touch me, she thought. No, she wouldn't remember that, not if she wanted to sleep tonight. Kate merely inclined her head in cool agreement. "I want to thank Marsh."

"You can thank him tomorrow." Ky dropped the waitress's tip on the table. "He's busy."

She started to protest, then saw Marsh disappear into what must have been the kitchen. "All right." Kate moved by him and out into the balmy evening air.

The sun was low, though it wouldn't set for nearly an hour. The clouds to the west were just touched with mauve and rose. When she stepped outside, Kate decided there were more people in the restaurant than there were on the streets.

A charter fishing boat glided into the harbor. Some of the tourists would be staying on the island, others would be riding back across Hatteras Inlet on one of the last ferries of the day.

She'd like to go out on the water now, while the light was softening and the breeze was quiet. Now, she thought, while others were coming in and the sea would stretch for mile after endless empty mile.

Shaking off the mood, she headed for the hotel. What she needed wasn't a sunset sail but a good solid night's sleep. Daydreaming was foolish, and tomorrow too important.

The same hotel. Ky glanced up at her window. He already knew she had the same room. He'd walked her there before, but then she'd have had her arm through his in that sweet way she had of joining them together. She'd have looked up and laughed at him over something that had happened that day. And she'd have kissed him, warm, long and lingeringly before the door would close behind her.

Because her thoughts had run the same gamut, Kate turned to him while they were still outside the hotel. "Thank you, Ky." She made a business out of shifting her purse strap on her arm. "There's no need for you to go any further out of your way."

"No, there isn't." He'd have something to take home with him that night, he thought with sudden, fierce impatience. And he'd leave her something to take up to the room where they'd had one long, glorious night. "But then we've always looked at needs from different angles." He cupped his hand around the back of her neck, holding firm as he felt her stiffen.

"Don't." She didn't back away. Kate told herself she didn't back away because to do so would make her seem vulnerable. And she was, feeling those long hard fingers play against her skin again.

"I think this is something you owe me," he told her in a voice so quiet it shivered on the air. "Maybe something I owe myself."

He wasn't gentle. That was deliberate. Somewhere inside him was a need to punish for what hadn't been—or perhaps what had. The mouth he crushed on hers hungered, the arms he wrapped around her demanded. If she'd forgotten, he thought grimly, this would remind her. And remind her.

With her arms trapped between them, he could feel her hands ball into tight fists. Let her hate him, loathe him. He'd rather that than cool politeness.

But God she was sweet. Sweet and as delicate as one of the frothy waves that lapped and spread along the shoreline. Dimly, distantly, he knew he could drown in her without a murmur or complaint.

She wanted it to be different. Oh, how she wanted it to be different so that she'd feel nothing. But she felt everything.

The hard, impatient mouth that had always thrilled and bemused her—it was the same. The lean restless body that fit so unerringly against her—no different. The scent that clung to him, sea and salt—hadn't changed. Always when he kissed her, there'd been the sounds of water or wind or gulls. That, too, remained constant. Behind them boats rocked gently in their slips, water against wood. A gull resting on pilings let out a long, lonely call. The light dimmed as the sun dropped closer to the sea. The flood of past feelings rose up to merge and mingle with the moment.

She didn't resist him. Kate had told herself she wouldn't give him the satisfaction of a struggle. But the command to her brain not to respond was lost in the thin clouds of dusk. She gave because she had to. She took because she had no choice.

His tongue played over hers and her fists uncurled until Kate's palms rested against his chest. So warm, so hard, so familiar. He kissed as he always had, with complete concentration, no inhibitions and little patience.

Time tumbled back and she was young and in love and foolish. Why, she wondered while her head swam, should that make her want to weep?

He had to let her go or he'd beg. Ky could feel it rising in him. He wasn't fool enough to plead for what was already gone. He wasn't strong enough to accept that he had to let go again. The tug-of-war going on inside him was fierce enough to make him moan. On the sound he pulled away from her, frustrated, infuriated, bewitched.

Taking a moment, he stared down at her. Her look was the same, he realized—that half surprised, half speculative look she'd given him after their first kiss. It disoriented him. Whatever he'd sought to prove, Ky knew now he'd only proven that he was still as much enchanted with her as he'd ever been. He bit back an oath, instead, giving her a half-salute as he walked away.

"Get eight hours of sleep," he ordered without turning around.

# Chapter Four

Some mornings the sun seemed to rise more slowly than others, as if nature wanted to show off her particular majesty just a bit longer. When she'd gone to bed, Kate had left her shades up knowing that the morning light would awaken her before the travel alarm beside her bed rang.

She took the dawn as a gift to herself, something individual and personal. Standing at the window, she watched it bloom. The first quiet breeze of morning drifted through the screen to run over her hair and face, through the thin material of her nightshirt, cool and promising. While she stood, Kate absorbed the colors, the light and the silent thunder of day breaking over water.

The lazy contemplation was far different from her structured routine of the past months and years. Mornings had been a time to dress, a time to run over her schedule and notes for the day's classes over two cups of coffee and a quick breakfast. She never had time to give herself the dawn, so she took it now.

She slept better than she'd expected, lulled by the quiet, exhausted by the days of traveling and the strain on her emotions. There'd been no dreams to haunt her from the time she'd turned back the sheets until the first light had fallen over her face. Then she rose quickly. There'd be no dreams now.

Kate let the morning wash over her with all its new promises, its beginnings. Today was the start. Everything, from the moment she'd taken out her father's papers until she'd seen Ky again, had been a prelude. Even the brief, torrid embrace of the night before had been no more than a ghost of the past. Today was the real beginning.

She dressed and went out into the morning.

Breakfast was impossible. The excitement she'd so meticulously held off was beginning to strain for freedom. The feeling that what she was doing was right was back with her. Whatever it took, whatever it cost her, she'd look for the gold her father had dreamed of. She'd follow his directions. If she found nothing, she'd have looked anyway.

In looking, Kate had come to believe she'd lay all her personal ghosts to rest.

Ky's kiss. It had been aching, disturbing as it had always been. She'd been absorbed, just as she'd always been. Though she knew she had to face both Ky and the past, she hadn't known it would be so frighteningly easy to go back—back to that dark, dreamy world where only he had taken her.

Now that she knew, now that she'd faced even that, Kate had to prepare to fight the wind.

He'd never forgiven her, she realized, for saying no. For bruising his pride. She'd gone back to her world when he'd asked her to stay in his. Asked her to stay, Kate remembered, without offering anything, not even a promise. If he'd given her that, no matter how casual or airy the promise might have been, she wouldn't have gone. She wondered if he knew that.

Perhaps he thought if he could make her lose herself to him again, the scales would be even. She wouldn't lose.

Kate stuck her hands into the pockets of her brief pleated shorts. No, she didn't intend to lose. If he had pressed her last night, if he'd known just how weakened she'd been by that one kiss...

But he wouldn't know, she told herself. She wouldn't weaken again. For the summer, she'd make the treasure her goal and her one ambition. She wouldn't leave the island empty-handed this time.

He was already on board the *Vortex*. Kate could see him stowing gear, his hair tousled by the breeze that flowed in from the sea. With only cut-offs and a sleeveless T-shirt between him and the sun she could see the muscles coil and relax, the skin gleam.

Magnificent. She felt the dull ache deep in her stomach and tried to rationalize it away. After all, a well-honed masculine build should make a woman respond. It was natural. One could even call it impersonal, Kate decided. As she started down the dock she wished she could believe it.

He didn't see her. A fishing boat already well out on the water had caught his attention. For a moment, she stopped, just watching him. Why was it she could always sense the restlessness in him? There was movement in him even when he was still, sound even when he was silent. What was it he saw when he looked out over the sea? Challenge? Romance?

He was a man who always seemed poised for action, for doing. Yet he could sit quietly and watch the waves as if there were nothing more important than that endless battle between earth and water.

Just now he stood on the deck of his boat, hands on hips, watching the tubby fishing vessel putt toward the horizon. It was something he'd seen countless times, yet he stopped to take it in again. Kate looked where Ky looked and wished she could see what he was seeing.

Quietly she went forward, her deck shoes making no sound, but he turned, eyes still intense. "You're early," he said, and with no more greeting reached out a hand to help her on board.

"I thought you might be as anxious to start as I am."

Palm met palm, rough against smooth. Both of them broke contact as soon as possible.

"It should be an easy ride." He looked back to sea, toward the boat, but this time he didn't focus on it. "The wind's coming in from the north, no more than ten knots."

"Good." Though it wouldn't have mattered to her nor, she thought, to him, if the wind had been twice as fast. This was the morning to begin.

She could sense the impatience in him, the desire to be gone and doing. Wanting to make things as simple as possible Kate helped Ky cast off, then walked to the stern. That would keep the maximum distance between them. They didn't speak. The engine roared to life, shattering the calm. Smoothly, Ky maneuvered the small cruiser out of the harbor, setting up a small wake that caused the water to lap against pilings. He kept the same steady even speed while they sailed through the shallows of Ocracoke Inlet. Looking back, Kate watched the distance between the boat and the village grow.

The dreamy quality remained. The last thing she saw was a child walking down a pier with a rod cocked rakishly over his shoulder. Then she turned her face to the sea.

Warm wind, glaring sun. Excitement. Kate hadn't been sure the feelings would be the same. But when she closed her eyes, letting the dull red light glow behind her lids, the salty mist touch her face, she knew this was a love that had remained constant, one that had waited for her.

Sitting perfectly still, she could feel Ky increase the speed until the boat was eating its way through the water as sleekly as a cat moves through the jungle. With her eyes closed, she enjoyed the movement, the speed, the sun. This was a thrill that had never faded. Tasting it again, she understood that it never would.

She'd been right, Kate realized, the hunt would be much more exciting than the final goal. The hunt, and no matter how cautious she was, the man at the helm.

He'd told himself he wouldn't look back at her. But he had to—just once. Eyes closed, a smile playing around her mouth, hair dancing around her face where the wind nudged it from the pins. It brought back a flash of memory—to the first time he'd seen her like that and realized he had to have her. She looked calm, totally at peace. He felt there was a war raging inside him that he had no control over.

Even when he turned back to sea again Ky could see her, leaning back against the stern, absorbing what wind and water offered. In defense, he tried to picture her in a classroom, patiently explaining the intricacies of *Don Juan* or *Henry IV*. It didn't help. He could only imagine her sitting behind him, soaking up sun and wind as if she'd been starved for it.

Perhaps she had been. Though she didn't know what direction Ky's thoughts had taken, Kate realized she'd never been further away from the classroom or the demands she placed on herself there than she was at this moment. She was part teacher, there was no question of that, but she was also, no matter how she'd tried to banish it, part dreamer.

With the sun and the wind on her skin, she was too exhilarated to be frightened by the knowledge, too content to worry. It was a wild, free sensation to experience again something known, loved, then lost.

Perhaps... Perhaps it was too much like the one frenzied kiss she'd shared with Ky the night before, but she needed it. It might be a foolish need, even a dangerous one. Just once, only this once, she told herself, she wouldn't question it.

Steady, strong, she opened her eyes again. Now she could watch the sun toss its diamonds on the surface of the water. They rippled, enticing, enchanting. The fishing boat Ky had watched move away from the island before them was anchored, casting its nets. A purse seiner, she remembered. Ky had explained the wide, weighted net to her once and how it was often used to haul in menhaden.

She wondered why he'd never chosen that life, where he could work and live on the water day after day. But not alone, she recalled with a ghost of a smile. Fishermen were their own community, on the sea and off it. It wasn't often Ky chose to share himself or his time with anyone. There were times, like this one, when she understood that perfectly.

Whether it was the freedom or the strength that was in her, Kate approached him without nerves. "It's as beautiful as I remember."

He dreaded having her stand beside him again. Now, however, he discovered the tension at the base of his neck had eased. "It doesn't change much." Together they watched the gulls swoop around the fishing boat, hoping for easy pickings. "Fishing's been good this year."

"Have you been doing much?"

"Off and on."

"Clamming?"

He had to smile when he remembered how she'd looked, jeans rolled up to her knees, bare feet full of sand as he'd taught her how to dig. "Yeah."

She, too, remembered, but her only memories were of warm days, warm nights. "I've often wondered what it's like on the island in winter."

"Quiet."

She took the single careless answer with a nod. "I've often wondered why you preferred that."

He turned to her, measuring. "Have you?"

Perhaps that had been a mistake. Since it had already been made, Kate shrugged. "It would be foolish of me to say I hadn't thought of the island or you at all during the last four years. You've always made me curious."

He laughed. It was so typical of her to put things that way. "Because all your tidy questions weren't answered. You think too much like a teacher, Kate."

"Isn't life a multiple choice?" she countered. "Maybe two or three answers would fit, but only one's ultimately right."

"No, only one's ultimately wrong." He saw her eyes take on that thoughtful, considering expression. She was, he knew, weighing the pros and cons of his statement. Whether she agreed or not, she'd consider all the angles. "You haven't changed either," he murmured.

"I thought the same of you. We're both wrong. Neither of us have stayed the same. That's as it should be." Kate looked away from him, further east, then gave a quick cry of pleasure. "Oh, look!" Without thinking, she put her hand on his arm, slender fingers gripping taut muscle. "Dolphins."

She watched them, a dozen, perhaps more, leap and dive in their musical pattern. Pleasure was touched with envy. To move like that, she thought, from water to air and back to water again. It was a freedom that might drive a man mad with the glory of it. But what a madness...

"Fantastic, isn't it?" she murmured. "To be part of the air and the sea. I'd nearly forgotten."

"How much?" Ky studied her profile until he could have etched the shape of it on the wind. "How much have you nearly forgotten?"

Kate turned her head, only then realizing just how close they stood. Unconsciously, she'd moved nearer to him when she'd seen the dolphins. Now she could see nothing but his face, inches from hers, feel nothing but the warm skin beneath her hand. His question, the depth of it, seemed to echo off the surface of the water to haunt her.

She stepped back. The drop before her was very deep and torn with rip tides. "All that was necessary," she said simply. "I'd like to look over my father's charts. Did you bring them on board?"

"Your briefcase is in the cabin." His hands gripped the wheel tightly, as though he were fighting against a storm. Perhaps he was. "You should be able to find your way below."

Without answering, Kate walked around him to the short steep steps that led below decks.

There were two narrow bunks with the spreads taut enough to bounce a coin if one was dropped. The galley just beyond would have all the essentials, she knew, in small, efficient scale. Everything would be in its place, as tidy as a monk's cell.

Kate could remember lying with Ky on one of the pristine bunks, flushed with passion while the boat swayed gently in the current and the music from his radio played jazz.

She gripped the leather of her case as if the pain in her fingers would help fight off the memories. To fight everything off entirely was too much to expect, but the intensity eased. Carefully she unfolded one of her father's charts and spread it on the bunk.

Like everything her father had done, the chart was precise and without frills. Though it had certainly not been his field, Hardesty had drawn a chart any sailor would have trusted.

It showed the coast of North Caroline, Pamlico Sound and the Outer Banks, from Manteo to Cape Lookout. As well as the lines of latitude and longitude, the chart also had the thin crisscrossing lines that marked depth.

Seventy-six degrees north by thirty-five degrees east. From the markings, that was the area her father had decided the *Liberty* had gone down. That was southeast of Ocracoke by no more than a few miles. And the depth... Yes, she decided as she frowned over the chart, the depth would still be considered shallow diving. She and Ky would have the relative freedom of wet suits and tanks rather than the leaded boots and helmets required for deep-sea explorations.

X marks the spot she thought, a bit giddy, but made herself fold the chart with the same care she'd used to open it. She felt the boat slow then heard the resounding silence when the engines shut off. A fresh tremor of anticipation went through her as she climbed the steps into the sunlight again.

Ky was already checking the tanks though she knew he would have gone over all the equipment thoroughly before setting out. "We'll go down here," he said as he rose from his crouched position. "We're about half a mile from the last place your father went in last summer."

In one easy motion he pulled off his shirt. Kate knew he was self aware, but he'd never been self-conscious. Ky had already stripped down to brief bikini trunks before she turned away for her own gear.

If her heart was pounding, it was possible to tell herself it was in anticipation of the dive. If her throat was dry, she could almost believe it was nerves at the thought of giving herself to the sea again. His body was hard and brown and lean, but she was only concerned with his skill and his knowledge. And he, she told herself, was only concerned with his fee and his twenty-five percent of the find.

She wore a snug tank suit under her shorts that clung to subtle curves and revealed long, slender legs that Ky knew were soft as water, strong as a runner's. He began to pull on the thin rubber wet suit. They were here to look for gold, to find a treasure that had been lost. Some treasures, he knew, could never be recovered.

As he thought of it, Ky glanced up to see Kate draw the pins from her hair. It fell, soft and slow, over, then past her shoulders. If she'd shot a dart into his chest, she couldn't have pierced his heart more accurately. Swearing under his breath, Ky lifted the first set of tanks.

"We'll go down for an hour today."

"But—"

"An hour's more than enough," he interrupted without sparing her a glance. "You haven't worn tanks in four years."

Kate slipped into the set he offered her, securing the straps until they were snug, but not tight. "I didn't tell you that."

"No, but you'd sure as hell have told me if you had." The corner of his mouth lifted when she remained silent. After attaching his own tanks, Ky climbed over the side onto the ladder. She could either argue, he figured, or she could follow.

To clear his mask, he spat into it, rubbed, then reached down to rinse it in salt water. Pulling it over his eyes and nose, Ky dropped into the sea. It took less than ten seconds before Kate plunged into the water beside him. He paused a moment, to make certain she didn't flounder or forget to breathe, then he headed for greater depth.

No, she wouldn't forget to breathe, but the first breath was almost a sigh as her body submerged. It was as thrilling to her as it had been the first time, this incredible ability to stay beneath the ocean's surface and breath air.

Kate looked up to see the sun spearing through the water, and held out a hand to watch the watery light play on her skin. She could have stayed there, she realized, just reveling in it. But with a curl of her body and a kick, she followed Ky into depth and dimness.

Ky saw a school of menhaden and wondered if they'd end up in the net of the fishing boat he'd watched that morning. When the fish swerved in a mass and rushed past him, he turned to Kate again. She'd been right when she'd told him she knew what to do. She swam as cleanly and as competently as ever.

He expected her to ask him how he intended to look for the *Liberty*, what plan he'd outlined. When she hadn't, Ky had figured it was for one of two reasons. Either she didn't want to have any in-depth conversation with him at the moment, or she'd already reasoned it out for herself. It seemed more likely to be the latter, as her mind was also as clean and competent as ever.

The most logical method of searching seemed to be a semi-circular route around Hardesty's previous dives. Slowly and methodically, they would widen the circle. If Hardesty had been right, they'd find the *Liberty* eventually. If he'd been wrong . . . they'd have spent the summer treasure hunting.

Though the tanks on her back reminded Kate not to take the weightless freedom for granted, she thought she could stay down forever. She wanted to touch—the water, the sea grass, the soft, sandy bottom. Reaching out toward a school of bluefish she watched them scatter defensively then regroup. She knew there were times when, as a diver moved through the dim, liquid world, he could forget the need for the sun. Perhaps Ky had been right in limiting the dive. She had to be careful not to take what she found again for granted.

The flattened disklike shape caught Ky's attention. Automatically, he reached for Kate's arm to stop her forward progress. The stingray that scuttled along the bottom looking for tasty crustaceans might be amusing to watch, but it was deadly. He gauged this one to be as long as he was tall with a tail as sharp and cruel as a razor. They'd give it a wide berth.

Seeing the ray reminded Kate that the sea wasn't all beauty and dreams. It was also pain and death. Even as she watched, the stingray struck out with its whiplike tail and caught a small, hapless bluefish. Once, then twice. It was nature, it was life. But she turned away. Through the protective masks, her eyes met Ky's.

She expected to see derision for an obvious weakness, or worse, amusement. She saw neither. His eyes were gentle, as they were very rarely. Lifting a hand, he ran his knuckles down her cheek, as he'd done years before when he'd chosen to offer comfort or affection. She felt the warmth, it reflected in her eyes. Then, as quickly as the moment had come, it was over. Turning, Ky swam away, gesturing for her to follow.

He couldn't afford to be distracted by those glimpses of vulnerability, those flashes of sweetness. They had already done him in once. Top priority was the job they'd set out to do. Whatever other plans he had, Ky intended to be in full control. When the time was right, he'd have his fill of Kate. That he promised himself. He'd take exactly what he felt she owed him. But she wouldn't touch his emotions again. When he took her to bed, it would be with cold calculation.

That was something else he promised himself.

Though they found no sign of the *Liberty*, Ky saw wreckage from other ships—pieces of metal, rusted, covered with barnacles. They might have been from a sub or a battleship from World War II. The sea absorbed what remained in her.

He was tempted to swim further out, but knew it would take twenty minutes to return to the boat. Circling around, he headed back, overlapping, double-checking the area they'd just covered.

Not quite a needle in a haystack, Ky mused, but close. Two centuries of storms and currents and sea quakes. Even if they had the exact location where the *Liberty* had sunk, rather than the last known location, it took calculation and guesswork, then luck to narrow the field down to a radius of twenty miles.

Ky believed in luck much the same way he imagined Hardesty had believed in calculation. Perhaps with a mixture of the two, he and Kate would find what was left of the *Liberty*.

Glancing over, he watched Kate gliding beside him. She was looking everywhere at once, but Ky didn't think her mind was on treasure or sunken ships. She was, as she'd been that summer before, completely enchanted with the sea and the life it held. He wondered if she still remembered all the information she'd demanded of him before the first dive. What about the physiological adjustments to the body? How was the $CO_2$ absorbed? What about the change in external pressure?

Ky felt a flash of humor as they started to ascend. He was dead sure Kate remembered every answer he'd given her, right down to the decimal point in pounds of pressure per square inch.

The sun caught her as she rose toward the surface, slowly. It shone around and through her hair, giving her an ethereal appearance as she swam straight up, legs kicking gently, face tilted toward sun and surface. If there were mermaids, Ky knew they'd look as she did—slim, long, with pale loose hair free in the water. A man could only hold onto a mermaid if he accepted the world she lived in as his own. Reaching out, he caught the tip of her hair in his fingers just before they broke the surface together.

Kate came up laughing, letting her mouthpiece fall and pushing her mask up. "Oh, it's wonderful! Just as I remembered." Treading water, she laughed again and Ky realized it was a sound he hadn't heard in four years. But he remembered it exactly.

"You looked like you wanted to play more than you wanted to look for sunken ships." He grinned at her, enjoying her pleasure and the ease of a smile he'd never expected to see again.

"I did." Almost reluctant, she reached out for the ladder to climb on board. "I never expected to find anything the first time down, and it was so wonderful just to dive again." She stripped off her tanks then checked the valves herself before she set them down. "Whenever I go down I begin to believe I don't need the sun anymore. Then when I come up it's warmer and brighter than I remember."

With the adrenaline still flowing, she peeled off her flippers, then her mask, to stand, face lifted toward the sun. "There's nothing else exactly like it."

"Skin diving." Ky tugged down the zipper of his wet suit. "I tried some in Tahiti last year. It's incredible being in that clear water with no equipment but a mask and flippers, and your own lungs."

"Tahiti?" Surprised and interested, Kate looked back as Ky stripped off the wet suit. "You went there?"

"Couple of weeks late last year." He dropped the wet suit in the big plastic can he used for storing equipment before rinsing.

"Because of your affection for islands?"

"And grass skirts."

The laughter bubbled out again. "I'm sure you'd look great in one."

He'd forgotten just how quick she could be when she relaxed. Because the gesture appealed, Ky reached over and gave her hair a quick tug. "I wish I'd taken snapshots." Turning, he jogged down the steps into the cabin.

"Too busy ogling the natives to put them on film for posterity?" Kate called out as she dropped down on the narrow bench on the starboard side.

"Something like that. And of course trying to pretend I didn't notice the natives ogling me."

She grinned. "People in grass skirts," she began then let out a muffled shout as he tossed a peach in her direction. Catching it cleanly, Kate smiled at him before she bit into the fruit.

"Still have good reflexes," Ky commented as he came up the last step.

"Especially when I'm hungry." She touched her tongue to her palm where juice dribbled. "I couldn't eat this morning, I was too keyed up."

He held out one of two bottles of cold soda he'd taken from the refrigerator. "About the dive?"

"That and..." Kate broke off, surprised that she was talking to him as if it had been four years before.

"And?" Ky prompted. Though his tone was casual, his gaze had sharpened.

Aware of it, Kate rose, turning away to look back over the stern. She saw nothing there but sky and water. "It was the morning," she murmured. "The way the sun came up over the water. All that color." She shook her head and water dripped from the ends of her hair onto the deck. "I haven't watched a sunrise in a very long time."

Making himself relax again, Ky leaned back, biting into his own peach as he watched her. "Why?"

"No time. No need."

"Do they both mean the same thing to you?"

Restless, she moved her shoulders. "When your life revolves around schedules and classes, I suppose one equals the other."

"That's what you want? A daily timetable?"

Kate looked back over her shoulder, meeting his eyes levelly. How could they ever understand each other, she wondered. Her world was as foreign to him as his to her. "It's what I've chosen."

"One of your multiple choices of life?" Ky countered, giving a short laugh before he tilted his bottle back again.

"Maybe, or maybe some parts of life only have one choice." She turned completely around, determined not to lose the euphoria that had come to her with the dive. "Tell me about Tahiti, Ky. What's it like?"

"Soft air, soft water. Blue, green, white. Those are the colors that come to mind, then outrageous splashes of red and orange and yellow."

"Like a Gauguin painting."

The length of the deck separated them. Perhaps that made it easier for him to smile. "I suppose, but I don't think he'd have appreciated all the hotels and resorts. It isn't an island that's been left to itself."

"Things rarely are."

"Whether they should be or not."

Something in the way he said it, in the way he looked at her, made Kate think he wasn't speaking of an island now, but of something more personal. She drank, cooling her throat, moistening her lips. "Did you scuba?"

"Some. Shells and coral so thick I could've filled a boat with them if I'd wanted. Fish that looked like they should've been in an aquarium. And sharks." He remembered one that had nearly caught him half a mile out. Remembering made him grin. "The waters off Tahiti are anything but boring."

Kate recognized the look, the recklessness that would always surface just under his skill. Perhaps he didn't look for trouble, but she thought he'd rarely sidestep it. No, she doubted they'd ever fully understand each other, if they had a lifetime.

"Did you bring back a shark's tooth necklace?"

"I gave it to Hope." He grinned again. "Linda won't let her have it yet."

"I should think not. Does it feel odd, being an uncle?"

"No. She looks like me."

"Ah, the male ego."

Ky shrugged, aware that he had a healthy share and was comfortable with it. "I get a kick out of watching her run Marsh and Linda in circles. There's not much entertainment on the island."

She tried to imagine Ky being entertained by something as tame as a baby girl. She failed. "It's strange," Kate said after a moment. "Coming back to find Marsh and Linda married and parents. When I left Marsh treated Linda like his little sister."

"Didn't your father keep you up on progress on the island?"

The smile left her eyes. "No."

Ky lifted a brow. "Did you ask?"

"No."

He tossed his empty bottle into a small barrel. "He hadn't told you anything about the ship either, about why he kept coming back to the island year after year."

She tossed her drying hair back from her face. It hadn't been put in the tone of a question. Still, she answered because it was simpler that way. "No, he never mentioned the *Liberty* to me."

"That doesn't bother you?"

The ache came, but she pushed it aside. "Why should it?" she countered. "He was entitled to his own life, his privacy."

"But you weren't."

She felt the chill come and go. Crossing the deck, Kate dropped her bottle beside Ky's before reaching for her shirt. "I don't know what you mean."

"You know exactly what I mean." He closed his hand over hers before she could pull the shirt on. Because it would've been cowardly to do otherwise, she lifted her head and faced him. "You know," he said again, quietly. "You just aren't ready to say it out loud yet."

"Leave it alone, Ky." Her voice trembled, and though it infuriated her, she couldn't prevent it. "Just leave it."

He wanted to shake her, to make her admit, so that he could hear, that she'd left him because her father had preferred it. He wanted her to say, perhaps sob, that she hadn't had the strength to stand up to the man who had shaped and molded her life to suit his values and wants.

With an effort, he relaxed his fingers. As he had before, Ky turned away with something like a shrug. "For now," he said easily as he went back to the helm. "Summer's just beginning." He started the engine before turning around for one last look. "We both know what can happen during a summer."

# Chapter Five

"The first thing you have to understand about Hope," Linda began, steadying a vase the toddler had jostled, "is that she has a mind of her own."

Kate watched the chubby black-haired Hope climb onto a wing-backed chair to examine herself in an ornamental mirror. In the fifteen minutes Kate had been in Linda's home, Hope hadn't been still a moment. She was quick, surprisingly agile, with a look in her eyes that made Kate believe she knew exactly what she wanted and intended to get it, one way or the other. Ky had been right. His niece looked like him, in more ways than one.

"I can see that. Where do you find the energy to run a restaurant, keep a home and manage a fireball?"

"Vitamins," Linda sighed. "Lots and lots of vitamins. Hope, don't put your fingers on the glass."

"Hope!" the toddler cried out, making faces at herself in the mirror. "Pretty, pretty, pretty."

"The Silver ego," Linda commented. "It never tarnishes."

With a chuckle, Kate watched Hope crawl backwards out of the chair, land on her diaper-padded bottom and begin to systematically destroy the tower of blocks she'd built a short time before. "Well, she is pretty. It only shows she's smart enough to know it."

"It's hard for me to argue that point, except when she's spread toothpaste all over the bathroom floor." With a contented sigh, Linda sat back on the couch. She enjoyed having Monday afternoons off to play with Hope and catch up on the dozens of things that went by the wayside when the restaurant demanded her time. "You've been here over a week now, and this is the first time we've been able to talk."

Kate bent over to ruffle Hope's hair. "You're a busy woman."

"So are you."

Kate heard the question, not so subtly submerged in the statement, and smiled. "You know I didn't come back to the island to fish and wade, Linda."

"All right, all right, the heck with being tactful." With a mother's skill, she kept her antenna honed on her active toddler and leaned toward Kate. "What *are* you and Ky doing out on his boat every day?"

With Linda, evasions were neither necessary nor advisable. "Looking for treasure," Kate said simply.

"Oh." Expressing only mild surprise, Linda saved a budding African violet from her daughter's curious fingers. "Blackbeard's treasure." She handed Hope a rubber duck in lieu of the plant. "My grandfather still tells stories about it. Pieces of eight, a king's ransom and bottles of rum. I always figured that it was buried on land."

Amused at the way Linda could handle the toddler without breaking rhythm, Kate shook her head. "No, not Blackbeard's."

There were dozens of theories and myths about where the infamous pirate had hidden his booty, and fantastic speculation on just how rich the trove was. Kate had never considered them any more than stories. Yet she supposed, in her own way, she was following a similar fantasy.

"My father'd been researching the whereabouts of an English merchant ship that sank off the coast here in the eighteenth century."

"Your father?" Instantly Linda's attention sharpened. She couldn't conceive of the Edwin Hardesty she remembered from summers past as a treasure searcher. "That's why he kept coming to the island every summer? I could never figure out why..." She broke off, grimaced, then plunged ahead. "I'm sorry, Kate, but he never seemed the type to take up scuba diving as a hobby, and I never once saw him with a fish. He certainly managed to keep what he was doing a secret."

"Yes, even from me."

"You didn't know?" Linda glanced over idly as Hope began to beat on a plastic bucket with a wooden puzzle piece.

"Not until I went through his papers a few weeks ago. I decided to follow through on what he'd started."

"And you came to Ky."

"I came to Ky." Kate smoothed the material of her thin summer skirt over her knees. "I needed a boat, a diver, preferably an islander. He's the best."

Linda's attention shifted from her daughter to Kate. There was simple understanding there, but it didn't completely mask impatience. "Is that the only reason you came to Ky?"

Needs rose up to taunt her. Memories washed up in one warm wave. "Yes, that's the only reason."

Linda wondered why Kate should want her to believe what Kate didn't believe herself. "What if I told you he's never forgotten you?"

Kate shook her head quickly, almost frantically. "Don't."

"I love him." Linda rose to distract Hope who'd discovered tossing blocks was more interesting than stacking them. "Even though he's a frustrating, difficult man. He's Marsh's brother." She set Hope in front of a small army of stuffed animals before she turned and smiled. "He's my brother. And you were the first mainlander I was ever really close to. It's hard for me to be objective."

It was tempting to pour out her heart, her doubts. Too tempting. "I appreciate that, Linda. Believe me, what was between Ky and me was over a long time ago. Lives change."

Making a neutral sound, Linda sat again. There were some people you didn't press. Ky and Kate were both the same in that area, however diverse they were otherwise. "All right. You know what I've been doing the past four years." She sent a long-suffering look in Hope's direction. "Tell me what your life's been like."

"Quieter."

Linda laughed. "A small border war would be quieter than life in this house."

"Earning my doctorate as early as I did took a lot of concentrated effort." She'd needed that one goal to keep herself level, to keep herself...calm. "When you're teaching as well it doesn't leave much time for anything else." Shrugging, she rose. It sounded so staid, she realized. So dull. She'd wanted to learn, she'd wanted to teach, but in and of itself, it sounded hollow.

There were toys spread all over the living room, tiny pieces of childhood. A tie was tossed carelessly over the back of a chair next to a table where Linda had dropped her purse. Small pieces of a marriage. Family. She wondered, with a panic that came and went quickly, how she would ever survive the empty house back in Connecticut.

"This past year at Yale has been fascinating and difficult." Was she defending or explaining? Kate wondered impatiently. "Strange, even though my father taught, I didn't realize that being a teacher is just as hard and demanding as being a student."

"Harder," Linda declared after a moment. "You have to have the answers."

"Yes." Kate crouched down to look at Hope's collection of stuffed animals. "I suppose that's part of the appeal, though. The challenge of either knowing the answer or reasoning it out, then watching it sink in."

"Hoping it sinks in?" Linda ventured.

Kate laughed again. "Yes, I suppose that's it. When it does, that's the most rewarding aspect. Being a mother can't be that much different. You're teaching every day."

"Or trying to," Linda said dryly.

"The same thing."

"You're happy?"

Hope squeezed a bright pink dragon then held it out for Kate. Was she happy? Kate wondered as she obliged by cuddling the dragon in turn. She'd been aiming for achievement, she supposed, not happiness. Her father had never asked that very simple, very basic question. She'd never taken the time to ask herself. "I want to teach," she answered at length. "I'd be unhappy if I couldn't."

"That's a roundabout way of answering without answering at all."

"Sometimes there isn't any yes or no."

"Ky!" Hope shouted so that Kate jolted, whipping her head around to the front door.

"No." Linda noted the reaction, but said nothing. "She means the dragon. He gave it to her, so it's Ky."

"Oh." She wanted to swear but managed to smile as she handed the baby back her treasured dragon. It wasn't reasonable that just his name should make her hands unsteady, her pulse unsteady, her thoughts unsteady. "He wouldn't pick the usual, would he?" she asked carelessly as she rose.

"No." She gave Kate a very direct, very level look. "His tastes have always run to the unique."

Amusement helped to relax her. Kate's brow rose as she met the look. "You don't give up, do you?"

"Not on something I believe in." A trace of stubbornness came through. The stubbornness, Kate mused, that had kept her determinedly waiting for Marsh to fall in love with her. "I believe in you and Ky," Linda continued. "You two can make a mess of it for as long as you want, but I'll still believe in you."

"You haven't changed," Kate said on a sigh. "I came back to find you a wife, a mother, and the owner of a restaurant, but you haven't changed at all."

"Being a wife and mother only makes me more certain that what I believe is right." She had her share of arrogance, too, and used it. "We don't own the restaurant," she added as an afterthought.

"No?" Surprised, Kate looked up again. "But I thought you said the Roost was yours and Marsh's."

"We run it," Linda corrected. "And we do have a twenty percent interest." Sitting back, she gave Kate a pleased smile. There was nothing she liked better than to drop small bombs in calm water and watch the ripples. "Ky owns the Roost."

"Ky?" Kate couldn't have disguised the astonishment if she'd tried. The Ky Silver she thought she knew hadn't owned anything but a boat and a shaky beach cottage. He hadn't wanted to. Buying a restaurant, even a small one on a remote island took more than capital. It took ambition.

"Apparently he didn't bother to mention it."

"No." He'd had several opportunities, Kate recalled, the night they'd had dinner. "No, he didn't. It doesn't seem characteristic," she murmured. "I can picture him buying another boat, a bigger boat or a faster boat, but I can't imagine him buying a restaurant."

"I guess it surprised everyone except Marsh—but then Marsh knows Ky better than anyone. A couple of weeks before we were married, Ky told us he'd bought the place and intended to remodel. Marsh was ferrying over to Hatteras every day to work, I was helping out in my aunt's craft shop during the season. When Ky asked if we wanted to buy in for twenty percent and take over as managers, we jumped at it." She smiled, pleased, and perhaps relieved. "It wasn't a mistake for any of us."

She remembered the homey atmosphere, the excellent sea food, the fast service. No, it hadn't been a mistake, but Ky... "I just can't picture Ky in business, not on land anyway."

"Ky knows the island," Linda said simply. "And he knows what he wants. To my way of thinking, he just doesn't always know how to get it."

Kate was going to avoid that area of speculation. "I'm going to take a walk down to the beach," she decided. "Would you like to come?"

"I'd love to, but—" With a gesture of her hand Linda indicated why Hope had been quiet for the last few minutes. With her arm hooked around her dragon, she was sprawled over the rest of the animals, sound asleep.

"It's either stop or go with her, isn't it?" Kate observed with a laugh.

"The nice thing is that when she stops, so can I." Expertly Linda gathered up Hope, cradling her daughter on her shoulder. "Have a nice walk, and stop into the Roost tonight if you have the chance."

"I will." Kate touched Hope's head, the thick, dark, disordered hair that was so much like her uncle's. "She's beautiful, Linda. You're very lucky."

"I know. It's something I don't ever forget."

Kate let herself out of the house and walked along the quiet street. Clouds were low, making the light gloomy, but the rain held off. She could taste it in the breeze, the clean freshness of it, mixed with the faintest hint of the sea. It was in that direction she walked.

On an island, she'd discovered, you were much more drawn to the water than to the land. It was the one thing she'd understood completely about Ky, the one thing she'd never questioned.

It had been easier to avoid going to the beach in Connecticut, though she'd always loved the rocky, windy New England coast. She'd been able to resist it, knowing what memories it would bring back. Pain. Kate had learned there were ways of avoiding pain. But here, knowing you could reach the edge of land by walking in any direction, she couldn't resist. It might have been wiser to walk to the sound, or the inlet. She walked to the sea.

It was warm enough that she needed no more than the sheer skirt and blouse, breezy enough so that the material fluttered around her. She saw two men, caps low over foreheads, their rods secured in the sand, talking together while they sat on buckets and waited for a strike. Their voices didn't carry above the roar and thunder of surf, but she knew their conversation would deal with bait and lures and yesterday's catch. She wouldn't disturb them, nor they her. It was the way of the islander to be friendly enough, but not intrusive.

The water was as gray as the sky, but she didn't mind. Kate had learned not just to accept its moods but to appreciate the contrasts of each one. When the sea was like this, brooding, with threats of violence on the surface, that meant a storm. She found it appealed to a restlessness in herself she rarely acknowledged.

Whitecaps tossed with systematic fever. The spray rose high and wide. The cry of gulls didn't seem lonely or plaintive now, but challenging. No, a gray gloomy sky meeting a gray sea was anything but dull. It teamed with energy. It boiled with life.

The wind tugged at her hair, loosening pins. She didn't notice. Standing just away from the edge of the surf, Kate faced wind and sea with her eyes wide. She had to think about what she'd just discovered about Ky. Perhaps what she had been determined not to discover about herself.

Thinking there, alone in the gray threatening light before a storm, was what Kate felt she needed. The constant wind blowing in from the east would keep her head clear. Maybe the smells and sounds of the sea would remind her of what she'd had and rejected, and what she'd chosen to have.

Once she'd had a powerful force that had held her swirling, breathless. That force was Ky, a man who could pull on your emotions, your senses, by simply being. The recklessness had attracted her once, the tough arrogance combined with unexpected gentleness. What she saw as his irresponsibility had disturbed her. Kate sensed that he was a man who would drift through life when she'd been taught from birth to seek out a goal and work for it to the exclusion of all else. It was that very different outlook on life that set them poles apart.

Perhaps he had decided to take on some responsibility in his life with the restaurant, Kate decided. If he had she was glad of it. But it couldn't make any difference. They were still poles apart.

She chose the calm, the ordered. Success was satisfaction in itself when success came from something loved. Teaching was vital to her, not just a job, not even a profession. The giving of knowledge fed her. Perhaps for a moment in Linda's cozy, cluttered home it hadn't seemed like enough. Not quite enough. Still, Kate knew if you wished for too much, you often received nothing at all.

With the wind whipping at her face she watched the rain begin far out to sea in a dark curtain. If the past had been a treasure she'd lost, no chart could take her back. In her life, she'd been taught only one direction.

Ky never questioned his impulses to walk on the beach. He was a man who was comfortable with his own mood swings, so comfortable, he rarely noticed them. He hadn't deliberately decided to stop work on his boat at a certain time. He simply felt the temptation of sea and storm and surrendered to it.

Ky watched the seas as he made his way up and over the hill of sand. He could have found his way without faltering in the dark, with no moon. He'd stood on shore and watched the rain at sea before, but repetition didn't lessen the pleasure. The wind would bring it to the island, but there was still time to seek shelter if shelter were desired. More often than not, Ky would let the rain flow over him while the waves rose and fell wildly.

He'd seen his share of tropical storms and hurricanes. While he might find them exhilarating, he appreciated the relative peace of a summer rain. Today he was grateful for it. It had given him a day away from Kate.

They had somehow reached a shaky, tense coexistence that made it possible for them to be together day after day in a relatively small space. The tension was making him nervy; nervy enough to make a mistake when no diver could afford to make one.

Seeing her, being with her, knowing she'd withdrawn from him as a person was infinitely more difficult than being apart from her. To Kate, he was only a means to an end, a tool she used in the same way he imagined she used a textbook. If that was a bitter pill, he felt he had only himself to blame. He'd accepted her terms. Now all he had to do was live with them.

He hadn't heard her laugh again since the first dive. He missed that, Ky discovered, every bit as much as he missed the taste of her lips, the feel of her in his arms. She wouldn't give him any of it willingly, and he'd nearly convinced himself he didn't want her any other way.

But at night, alone, with the sound of the surf in his head, he wasn't sure he'd survive another hour. Yet he had to. It was the fierce drive for survival that had gotten him through the last years. Her rejection had eaten away at him, then it had pushed him to prove something to himself. Kate had been the reason for his risking every penny he'd had to buy the Roost. He'd needed something tangible. The Roost had given him that, in much the same way the charter boat he'd recently bought gave him a sense of worth he once thought was unnecessary.

So he owned a restaurant that made a profit, and a boat that was beginning to justify his investment. It had given his innate love of risk an outlet. It wasn't money that mattered, but the dealing, the speculation, the possibilities. A search for sunken treasure wasn't much different.

What was she looking for really? Ky wondered. Was the gold her objective? Was she simply looking for an unusual way to spend her holiday? Was she still trying to give her father the blind devotion he'd expected all her life? Was it the hunt? Watching the wall of rain move slowly closer, Ky found of all the possibilities he wanted it to be the last.

With perhaps a hundred yards between them, both Kate and Ky looked out to the sea and the rain without being aware of each other. He thought of her and she of him, but the rain crept closer and time slipped by. The wind grew bolder. Both of them could admit to the restlessness that churned inside them, but neither could acknowledge simple loneliness.

Then they turned to walk back up the dunes and saw each other.

Kate wondered how long he'd been there, and how, when she could feel the waves of tension and need, she hadn't known the moment he'd stepped onto the beach. Her mind, her body—always so calm and cooperative—sprang to fevered life when she saw him. Kate knew she couldn't fight that, only the outcome. Still she wanted him. She told herself that just wanting was asking for disaster, but that didn't stop the need. If she ran from him now she'd admit defeat. Instead Kate took the first step across the sand toward him.

The thin white cotton of her skirt flapped around her, billowing, then clinging to the slender body he already knew. Her skin seemed very pale, her eyes very dark. Again Ky thought of mermaids, of illusions and of foolish dreams.

"You always liked the beach before a storm," Kate said when she reached him. She couldn't smile though she told herself she would. She wanted, though she told herself she wouldn't.

"It won't be much longer." He hooked his thumbs into the front pockets of his jeans. "If you didn't bring your car, you're going to get wet."

"I was visiting Linda." Kate turned her head to look back at the rain. No, it wouldn't be much longer. "It doesn't matter," she murmured. "Storms like this are over just as quickly as they begin." Storms like this, she thought, and like others. "I met Hope. You were right."

"About what?"

"She looks like you." This time she did manage to smile, though the tension was balled at the base of her neck. "Did you know she named a doll after you?"

"A dragon's not a doll," Ky corrected. His lips curved. He could resist a great deal, be apathetic about a great deal more, but he found it virtually impossible to do either when it came to his niece. "She's a great kid. Hell of a sailor."

"You take her out on your boat?"

He heard the astonishment and shrugged it away. "Why not? She likes the water."

"I just can't picture you..." Breaking off, Kate turned back to the sea again. No, she couldn't picture him entertaining a child with toy dragons and boat rides, just as she couldn't picture him in the business world with ledgers and accountants. "You surprise me," she said a bit more casually. "About a lot of things."

He wanted to reach out and touch her hair, wrap those loose blowing ends around his finger. He kept his hands in his pockets. "Such as?"

"Linda told me you own the Roost."

He didn't have to see her face to know it would hold that thoughtful, considering expression. "That's right, or most of it anyway."

"You didn't mention it when we were having dinner there."

"Why should I?" She didn't have to see him to know he shrugged. "Most people don't care who owns a place as long as the food's good and the service is quick."

"I guess I'm not most people." She said it quietly, so quietly the words barely carried over the sound of the waves. Even so, Ky tensed.

"Why would it matter to you?"

Before she could think, she turned back, her eyes full of emotion. "Because it all matters. The whys, the hows. Because so much has changed and so much is the same. Because I want..." Breaking off, she took a step back. The look in her eyes turned to panic just before she started to dash away.

"What?" Ky demanded, grabbing her arm. "What do you want?"

"I don't know!" she shouted, unaware that it was the first time she'd done so in years. "I don't know what I want. I don't understand why I don't."

"Forget about understanding." He pulled her closer, holding her tighter when she resisted—or tried to. "Forget everything that's not here and now." The nights of restlessness and frustration already had his mercurial temperament on edge. Seeing her when he hadn't expected to made his emotions teeter. "You walked away from me once, but I won't crawl for you again. And you," he added with his eyes suddenly dark, his face suddenly close, "you damn well won't walk away as easy this time, Kate. Not this time."

With his arms wrapped around her he held her against him. His lips hovered above hers, threatening, promising. She couldn't tell. She didn't care. It was their taste she wanted, their pressure, no matter how harsh, how demanding. No matter what the consequence. Intellect and emotion might battle, and the battle might be eternal. Yet as she stood there crushed against him, feeling the wind whip at both of them, she already knew what the inevitable outcome would be.

"Tell me what you want, Kate." His voice was low, but as demanding as a shout. "Tell me what you want—now."

Now, she thought. If there could only be just now. She started to shake her head, but his breath feathered over her skin. That alone made future and past fade into insignificance.

"You," she heard herself murmur. "Just you." Reaching up she drew his face down to hers.

A wild passionate wind, a thunderous surf, the threat of rain just moments away. She felt his body—hard and confident against hers. She tasted his lips—soft, urgent. Over the thunder in her head and the thunder to the east, she heard her own moan. She wanted, as long as the moment lasted.

His tongue tempted; she surrendered to it. He dove deep and took all, then more. It might never be enough. With no hesitation, Kate met demand with demand, heat with heat. While mouth sought mouth, her hands roamed his face, teaching what she hadn't forgotten, reacquainting her with the familiar.

His skin was rough with a day's beard, the angle of cheek and jaw, hard and defined. As her fingers inched up she felt the soft brush of his hair blown by the wind.

The contrast made her tremble before she dove her fingers deeper.

She could make him blind and deaf with needs. Knowing it, Ky couldn't stop it. The way she touched him, so sure, so sweet while her mouth was molten fire. Desire boiled in him, rising so quickly he was weak with it before his mind accepted what his body couldn't deny. He held her closer, hard against soft, rough against smooth, flame against flame.

Through the thin barrier of her blouse he felt her flesh warm to his touch. He knew the skin here would be delicate, as fragile as the underside of a rose. The scent would be as sweet, the taste as honeyed. Memories, the moment, the dream of more, all these combined to make him half mad. He knew what it would be like to have her, and knowing alone aroused. He felt her now, and feeling made him irrational.

He wanted to take her right there, next to the sea, while the sky opened up and poured over them.

"I want you." With his face buried against her neck he searched for all the places he remembered. "You know how much. You always knew."

"Yes." Her head was spinning. Every touch, every taste added speed to the whirl. Whatever doubts she'd had, Kate had never doubted the want. She hadn't always understood it, the intensity of it, but she'd never doubted it. It was pulling at her now—his, hers—the mutual, mindless passion they'd always been able to ignite in one another. She knew where it would lead—to dark, secret places full of sound and velocity. Not the eye of the hurricane, never the calm with him, but full fury from beginning to end. She knew where it would lead, and knew there'd be glory and freedom. But Ky had spoken no less than the truth when he'd said she wouldn't walk away so easily this time. It was that truth that made her reach for reason, when it would have been so simple to reach for madness.

"We can't." Breathless, she tried to turn in his arms. "Ky, *I* can't." This time when she took his face in her hands it was to draw it away from hers. "This isn't right for me."

Fury mixed with passion. It showed in his eyes, in the press of his fingers on her arms. "It's right for you. It's never been anything but right for you."

"No." She had to deny it, she had to mean it, because he was so persuasive. "No, it's not. I've always been attracted to you. It'd be ridiculous for me to try to pretend otherwise, but this isn't what I want for myself."

His fingers tightened. If they brought her pain neither of them acknowledged it. "I told you to tell me what you wanted. You did."

As he spoke the sky opened, just as he'd imagined. Rain swept in from the sea, tasting of salt, the damp wind and mystery. Instantly drenched, they stood just as they were, close, distant, with his hands firm on her arms and hers light on his face. She felt the water wash over her body, watched it run over his. It stirred her. She couldn't say why, she wouldn't give in to it.

"At that moment I did want you, I can't deny it."

"And now?" he demanded.

"I'm going back to the village."

"Damn it, Kate, what else do you want?"

She stared at him through the rain. His eyes were dark, stormy as the sea that raged behind him. Somehow he was more difficult to resist when he was like this, volatile, on edge, not quite controlled. She felt desire knot in her stomach, and swim in her head. That was all, Kate told herself. That was all it had ever been. Desire without understanding. Passion without future. Emotion without reason.

"Nothing you can give me," she whispered, knowing she'd have to dig for the strength to walk away, dig for it even to take the first step. "Nothing we can give to each other." Dropping her hands she stepped back. "I'm going back."

"You'll come back to me," Ky said as she took the first steps from him. "And if you don't," he added in a tone that made her hesitate, "it won't make any difference. We'll finish what's been started again."

She shivered, but continued to walk. Finish what's been started again. That was what she most feared.

# Chapter Six

The storm passed. In the morning the sea was calm and blue, sprinkled with diamonds of sunlight from a sky where all clouds had been whisked away. It was true that rain freshened things—the air, grass, even the wood and stone of buildings.

The day was perfect, the wind calm. Kate's nerves rolled and jumped.

She'd committed herself to the project. It was her agreement with Ky that forced her to go to the harbor as she'd been doing every other morning. It made her climb on deck when she wanted nothing more than to pack and leave the island the way she'd come. If Ky could complete the agreement after what had passed between them on the beach, so could she.

Perhaps he sensed the fatigue she was feeling, but he made no comment on it. They spoke only when necessary as he headed out to open sea. Ky stood at the helm, Kate at the stern. Still, even the roar of the engine didn't disguise the strained silence. Ky checked the boat's compass, then cut the engines. Silence continued, thunderously.

With the deck separating them, each began to don their equipment—wet suits, the weight belts that would give them neutral buoyancy in the water, headlamps to light the sea's dimness, masks for sight. Ky checked his depth gauge and compass on his right wrist, then the luminous dial of the watch on his left while Kate attached the scabbard for her diver's knife onto her leg just below the knee.

Without speaking, they checked the valves and gaskets on the tanks, then strapped them on, securing buckles. As was his habit, Ky went into the water first, waiting until Kate joined him. Together they jackknifed below the surface.

The familiar euphoria reached out for her. Each time she dived, Kate expected the underwater world to become more commonplace. Each time it was still magic. She acknowledged what made it possible for her to join creatures of the sea—the regulator with its mouthpiece and hose that brought her air from the tanks on her back, the mask that gave her visibility. She knew the importance of every gauge. She acknowledged the technology, then put it in the practical side of her brain while she simply enjoyed.

They swam deeper, keeping in constant visual contact. Kate knew Ky often dived alone, and that doing so was always a risk. She also knew that no matter how much anger and resentment he felt toward her, she could trust him with her life.

She relied on Ky's instincts as much as his ability. It was his expertise that guided her now, perhaps more than her father's careful research and calculations. They were combing the very edge of the territory her father had mapped out, but Kate felt no discouragement. If she hadn't trusted Ky's skill and instincts, she would never have come back to Ocracoke.

They were going deeper now than they had on their other dives. Kate equalized by letting a tiny bit of air into her suit. Feeling the "squeeze" on her eardrums at the change in pressure, she relieved it carefully. A damaged eardrum could mean weeks without being able to dive.

When Ky signaled for her to switch on her head lamp she obeyed without question. Excitement began to rise.

The sunlight was fathoms above them. The world here never saw it. Sea grass swayed in the current. Now and then a fish, curious and brave enough, would swim along beside them only to vanish in the blink of an eye at a sudden movement.

Ky swam smoothly through the water, using his feet to propel him at a steady pace. Their lamps cut through the murk, surprising more fish, illuminating rock formations that had existed under the sea for centuries. Kate discovered shapes and faces in them.

No, she could never dive alone, Kate decided as Ky slowed his pace to keep rhythm with her more meandering one. It was so easy for her to lose her sense of time and direction. Air came into her lungs with a simple drawing of breath as long as the tanks held oxygen, but the gauges on her wrist only worked if she remembered to look at them.

Even mortality could be forgotten in enchantment. And enchantment could too easily lead to a mistake. It was a lesson she knew, but one that could slip away from her. The timelessness, the freedom was seductive. The feeling was somehow as sensual as the timeless freedom felt in a lover's arms. Kate knew this pleasure could be as dangerous as a lover, but found it as difficult to resist.

There was so much to see, to touch. Crustaceans of different shapes, sizes and hues. They were alive here in their own milieu, so different from when they washed up helplessly on the beach for children to collect in buckets. Fish swam in and out of waving grass that would be limp and lifeless on land. Unlike dolphins or man, some creatures would never know the thrill of both air and water.

Her beam passed over another formation, crusted with barnacles and sea life. She nearly passed it, but curiosity made her turn back so that the light skimmed over it a second time. Odd, she thought, how structured some of the shapes could be. It almost looked like...

Hesitating, using her arms to reverse her progress, Kate turned in the water to play her light over the shape from end to end. Excitement rose so quickly she grabbed Ky's arm in a grip strong enough to make him stop to search for a defect in her equipment. With a shake of her head Kate warded him off, then pointed.

When their twin lights illuminated the form on the ocean floor, Kate nearly shouted with the discovery. It wasn't a shelf of rock. The closer they swam toward it the more apparent that became. Though it was heavily corroded and covered with crustaceans, the shape of the cannon remained recognizable.

Ky swam around the barrel. When he removed his knife and struck the cannon with the hilt the metallic sound rang out strangely. Kate was certain she'd never heard anything more musical. Her laughter came out in a string of bubbles that made Ky look in her direction and grin.

They'd found a corroded cannon, he thought, and she was as thrilled as if they'd found a chest full of doubloons. And he understood it. They'd found something perhaps no one had seen for two centuries. That in itself was a treasure.

With a movement of his hand he indicated for her to follow, then they began to swim slowly east. If they'd found a cannon, it was likely they'd find more.

Reluctant to leave her initial discovery, Kate swam with him, looking back as often as she looked ahead. She hadn't realized the excitement would be this intense. How could she explain what it felt like to discover something that had lain untouched on the sea floor for more than two centuries? Who would understand more clearly, she wondered, her colleagues at Yale or Ky? Somehow she felt her colleagues would understand intellectually, but they would never understand the exhilaration. Intellectual pleasure didn't make you giddy enough to want to turn somersaults.

How would her father have felt if he'd found it? She wished she knew. She wished she could have given him that one instant of exultation, perhaps shared it with him as they'd so rarely shared anything. He'd only known the planning, the theorizing, the bookwork. With one long look at that ancient weapon, she'd known so much more.

When Ky stopped and touched her shoulders, her emotions were as mixed as her thoughts. If she could have spoken she'd have told him to hold her, though she wouldn't have known why. She was thrilled, yet running through the joy was a thin shaft of sorrow—for what was lost, she thought. For what she'd never be able to find again.

Perhaps he knew something of what moved her. They couldn't communicate with words, but he touched her cheek—just a brush of his finger over her skin. It was more comforting to her than a dozen soft speeches.

She understood then that she'd never stopped loving him. No matter how many years, how many miles had separated them, what life she had she'd left with him. The time in between had been little more than existence. It was possible to live with emptiness, even to be content with it until you had that heady taste of life again.

She might have panicked. She might have run if she hadn't been trapped there, fathoms deep in the midst of a discovery. Instead she accepted the knowledge, hoping that time would tell her what to do.

He wanted to ask her what was going through her mind. Her eyes were full of so many emotions. Words would have to wait. Their time in the sea was almost up. He touched her face again and waited for the smile. When she gave it to him, Ky pointed at something behind her that he had just noticed moments before.

An oaken plank, old, splintered and bumpy with parasites. For the second time Ky removed his knife and began to pry the board from its bed. Silt floated up thinly, cutting visibility before it settled again. Replacing his knife, Ky gave the thumbs-up signal that meant they'd surface. Kate shook her head indicating that they should continue to search, but Ky merely pointed to his watch, then again to the surface.

Frustrated with the technology that allowed her to dive, but also forced her to seek air again, Kate nodded.

They swam west, back toward the boat. When she passed the cannon again, Kate felt a quick thrill of pride. She'd found it. And the discoveries were only beginning.

The moment her head was above water, she started to laugh. "We found it!" She grabbed the ladder with one hand as Ky began to climb up, placing his find and his tanks on the deck first. "I can't believe it, after hardly more than a week. It's incredible, that cannon lying down there all these years." Water ran down her face but she didn't notice. "We have to find the hull, Ky." Impatient, she released her tanks and handed them up to him before she climbed aboard.

"The chances are good—eventually."

"Eventually?" Kate tossed her wet hair out of her eyes. "We found this in less than a week." She indicated the board on the deck. She crouched over it, just wanting to touch. "We found the *Liberty*."

"We found a wreck," he corrected. "It doesn't have to be the *Liberty*."

"It is," she said with a determination that caused his brow to lift. "We found the cannon and this just on the edge of the area my father had charted. It all fits too well."

"Regardless of what wreck it is, it's undocumented. You'll get your name in the books, professor."

Annoyed she rose. They stood facing each other on either side of the plank they'd lifted out of the sea. "I don't care about having my name in the books."

"Your father's name then." He unzipped his wet suit to let his skin dry.

She remembered her feelings after spotting the cannon, how Ky had seemed to understand them. Could they only be kind to each other, only be close to each other, fathoms under the surface? "Is there something wrong with that?"

"Only if it's an obsession. You always had a problem with your father."

"Because he didn't approve of you?" she shot back.

His eyes took on that eerily calm, almost flat expression that meant his anger was lethal. "Because it mattered too much to you what he approved of."

That stung. The truth often did. "I came here to finish my father's project," she said evenly. "I made that clear from the beginning. You're still getting your fee."

"You're still following directions. His directions." Before she could retort, he turned toward the cabin. "We'll eat and rest before we go back under."

With an effort, she held onto her temper. She wanted to dive again, badly. She wanted to find more. Not for her father's approval, Kate thought fiercely. Certainly not for Ky's. She wanted this for herself. Pulling down the zipper of her wet suit, she went down the cabin steps.

She'd eat because strength and energy were vital to a diver. She'd rest for the same reason. Then, she determined, she'd go back to the wreck and find proof that it was the *Liberty*.

Calmer, she watched Ky go through a small cupboard. "Peanut butter?" she asked when she saw the jar he pulled out.

"Protein."

Her laugh helped her to relax again. "Do you still eat it with bananas?"

"It's still good for you."

Though she wrinkled her nose at the combination, she reminded herself that beggars couldn't be choosers. "When we find the treasure," she said recklessly, "I'll buy you a bottle of champagne."

Their fingers brushed as he handed her the first sandwich. "I'll hold you to it." He picked up his own sandwich and a quart of milk. "Let's eat on deck."

He wasn't certain if he wanted the sun or the space, but it wasn't any easier to be with her in that tiny cabin than it had been the first time, or the last. Taking her assent for granted, Ky went up the stairs again, without looking back. Kate followed.

"It might be good for you," Kate commented as she took the first bite, "but it still tastes like something you give five-year-olds when they scrape their knees."

"Five-year-olds require a lot of protein."

Giving up, Kate sat cross-legged on the deck. The sun was bright, the movement of the boat gentle. She wouldn't let his digs get to her, nor would she dig back. They were in this together, she reminded herself. Tension and sniping wouldn't help them find what they sought.

"It's the *Liberty*, Ky," she murmured, looking at the plank again. "I know it is."

"It's possible." He stretched out with his back against the port side. "But there are a lot of wrecks, unidentified and otherwise, all through these waters. Diamond Shoals is a graveyard."

"Diamond Shoals is fifty miles north."

"And the entire coastline along these barrier islands is full of littoral currents, rip currents and shifting sand ridges. Two hundred years ago they didn't have modern navigational devices. Hell, they didn't even have the lighthouses until the nineteenth century. I couldn't even give you an educated guess as to how many ships went down from the time Columbus set out until World War II."

Kate took another bite. "We're only concerned with one ship."

"Finding one's no big problem," he returned. "Finding a specific one's something else. Last year, after a couple of hurricanes breezed through, they found wrecks uncovered on the beach on Hatteras. There are plenty of houses on the island that were built from pieces of wreckage like that." He pointed to the plank with the remains of his sandwich.

Kate frowned at the board again. "It could be the *Liberty* just as easily as it couldn't."

"All right." Appreciating her stubbornness, Ky grinned. "But whatever it is, there might be treasure. Anything lost for more than two hundred years is pretty much finders keepers."

She didn't want to say that it wasn't any treasure she wanted. Just the *Liberty*'s. From what he said before, Kate was aware he already understood that. It was simply different for him. She took a long drink of cold milk. "What do you plan to do with your share?"

With his eyes half closed, he shrugged. He could do as he pleased now, a cache of gold wouldn't change that. "Buy another boat, I imagine."

"With what two-hundred-year-old gold would be worth today, you'd be able to buy a hell of a boat."

He grinned, but kept his eyes shaded. "I intend to. What about you?"

"I'm not sure." She wished she had some tangible goal for the money, something exciting, even fanciful. It just didn't seem possible to think beyond the hunt yet. "I thought I might travel a bit."

"Where?"

"Greece maybe. The islands."

"Alone?"

The food and the motion of the boat lulled her. She made a neutral sound as she shut her eyes.

"Isn't there some dedicated teacher you'd take with you? Someone you could discuss the Trojan War with?"

"Mmm, I don't want to go to Greece with a dedicated teacher."

"Someone else?"

"There's no one."

Sitting on the deck with her face lifted, her hair blowing, she looked like a finely crafted piece of porcelain. Something a man might look at, admire, but not touch. When her eyes were open, hot, her skin flushed with passion, he burned for her. When she was like this, calm, distant, he ached. He let the needs run through him because he knew there was no stopping them.

"Why?"

"Hmm?"

"Why isn't there anyone?"

Lazily she opened her eyes. "Anyone?"

"Why don't you have a lover?"

The sleepy haze cleared from her eyes instantly. He saw her fingers tense on the dark blue material that stretched snugly over her knees. "It's none of your business whether I do or not."

"You've just told me you don't."

"I told you there's no one I'd travel with," she corrected, but when she started to rise, he put a hand on her shoulder.

"It's the same thing."

"No, it's not, but it's still none of your business, Ky, any more than your personal life is mine."

"I've had women," he said easily. "But I haven't had a lover since you left the island."

She felt the pain and the pleasure sweep up through her. It was dangerous to dwell on the sensation. As dangerous as it was to lose yourself deep under the ocean. "Don't." She lifted her hand to remove his from her shoulder. "This isn't good for either of us."

"Why?" His fingers linked with hers. "We want each other. We both know the rules this time around."

Rules. No commitment, no promises. Yes, she understood them this time, but like mortality during a dive, they could easily be forgotten. Even now, with his eyes on hers, her fingers caught in his, the structure of those rules became dimmer and dimmer. He would hurt her again. There was never any question of that. Somehow, in the last twenty-four hours, it had become a matter of *how* she would deal with the pain, not *if*.

"Ky, I'm not ready." Her voice was low, not pleading, but plainly vulnerable. Though she wasn't aware of it, there was no defense she could put to better use.

He drew her up so that they were both standing, touching only hand to hand. Though she was tall, her slimness made her appear utterly fragile. It was that and the way she looked at him, with her head tilted back so their eyes could meet, that prevented him from taking what he was determined to have, without questions, without her willingness. Ruthlessly, that was how he told himself he wanted to take her, even though he knew he couldn't.

"I'm not a patient man."

"No."

He nodded, then released her hand while he still could. "Remember it," he warned before he turned to go to the helm. "We'll take the boat east, over the wreck and dive again."

An hour later they found a piece of rigging, broken and corroded, less than three yards from the cannon. By hand signals, Ky indicated that they'd start a stock-pile of the salvage. Later they'd come back with the means of bringing it up. There were more planks, some too big for a man to carry up, some small enough for Kate to hold in one hand.

When she found a pottery bowl, miraculously unbroken, she realized just what an archaeologist must feel after hours of digging when he unearths a fragment of another era. Here it was, cupped in her hand, a simple bowl, covered with silt, covered with age. Someone had eaten from it once, a seaman, relaxing briefly below deck perhaps on his first voyage across the Atlantic to the New World. His last journey in any event, Kate mused as she turned the bowl over in her hand.

The rigging, the cannon, the planks equaled ship. The bowl equaled man.

Though she put the bowl with the other pieces of their find, she intended to take it up with her on this dive. Whatever other artifacts they found could go to a museum, but the first, she'd keep.

They found pieces of glass that might have come from bottles that held whiskey, chunks of crockery that hadn't survived intact like the bowl. Bits of cups, bowls, plates littered the sea floor.

The galley, she decided. They must have found the galley. Over the years, the water pressure would have simply disintegrated the ship until it was all pieces spread on and under the floor of the ocean. It would, in essence, have become part of the sea, a home for the creatures and plant life that dwelt there.

But they'd found the galley. If they could find something, just one thing with the ship's name inscribed on it, they'd be certain.

Diligently, using her knife as a digging tool, Kate worked at the floor of the sea. It wasn't a practical way to search, but she saw no harm in trying her luck. They'd found crockery, glass, the unbroken bowl. Even as she glanced up she saw Ky examining what might have been half a dinner plate.

When she unearthed a long wooden ladle, Kate found that her excitement increased. They *had* found the galley, and in time, she'd prove to Ky that they'd found the *Liberty*.

Engrossed in her find, she turned to signal to Ky and moved directly into the path of a stingray.

He saw it. Ky was no more than a yard from Kate when the movement of the ray unearthing itself from its layer of sand and silt had caught his eye. His movement was pure reflex, done without thought or plan. He was quick. But even as he grabbed Kate's hand to swing her back behind him, out of range, the wicked, saw-toothed tail lashed out.

Her scream was muffled by the water, but the sound went through Ky just as surely as the stingray's poison went through Kate. Her body went stiff against his, rigid in pain and shock. The ladle she'd found floated down, out of her grip, until it landed silently on the bottom.

He knew what to do. No rational diver goes down unless he has a knowledge of how to handle an emergency. Still Ky felt a moment of panic. This wasn't just another diver, it was Kate. Before his mind could clear, her stiffened body went limp against him. Then he acted.

Cool, almost mechanically, he tilted her head back with the chin carry to keep her air passage open. He held her securely, pressing his chest into her tanks, keeping his hand against her ribcage. It ran through his mind that it was best she'd fainted. Unconscious she wouldn't struggle as she might had she been awake and in pain. It was best she'd fainted because he couldn't bear to think of her in pain. He kicked off for the surface.

On the rise he squeezed her, hard, forcing expanding air out of her lungs. There was always the risk of embolism. They were going up faster than safety allowed. Even while he ventilated his own lungs, Ky kept a lookout. She would bleed, and blood brought sharks.

The minute they surfaced, Ky released her weight belt. Supporting her with his arm wrapped around her, his hand grasping the ladder, Ky unhooked his tanks, slipped them over the side of the boat, then removed Kate's. Her face was waxy, but as he pulled the mask from her face she moaned. With that slight sound of life some of the blood came back to his own body. With her draped limply over his shoulder, he climbed the ladder onto the *Vortex*.

He laid her down on the deck, and with hands that didn't hesitate, began to pull the wet suit from her. She moaned again when he drew the snug material over the wound just above her ankle, but she didn't reach the surface of consciousness. Grimly, Ky examined the laceration the ray had caused. Even through the protection of her suit, the tail had penetrated deep into her skin. If Ky had only been quicker...

Cursing himself, Ky hurried to the cabin for the first aid kit.

As consciousness began to return. Kate felt the ache swimming up from her ankle to her head. Spears of pain shot through her, sharp enough to make her gasp and struggle, as if she could move away from it and find ease again.

"Try to lie still."

The voice was gentle and calm. Kate balled her hands into fists and obeyed it. Opening her eyes, she stared up at the pure blue sky. Her mind whirled with confusion, but she stared at the sky as though it were the only tangible thing in her life. If she concentrated, she could rise above the hurt. The ladle. Opening her hand she found it empty, she'd lost the ladle. For some reason it seemed vital that she have it.

"We found the galley." Her voice was hoarse with anguish, but her one hand remained open and limp. "I found a ladle. They'd have used it for spooning soup into that bowl. The bowl—it wasn't even broken. Ky..." Her voice weakened with a new flood of sensation as memory began to return. "It was a stingray. I wasn't watching for it, it just seemed to be there. Am I going to die?"

"No!" His answer was sharp, almost angry. Bending over her, he placed both hands on her shoulders so that she'd look directly into his face. He had to be sure she understood everything he said. "It was a stingray," he confirmed, not adding that it had been a good ten feet long. "Part of the spine's broken off, lodged just above your ankle."

He watched her eyes cloud further, part pain, part fear. His hands tightened on her shoulders. "It's not in deep. I can get it out, but it'll hurt like hell."

She knew what he was saying. She could stay as she was until he got her back to the doctor on the island, or she could trust him to treat her now. Though her lips trembled, she kept her eyes on his and spoke clearly.

"Do it now."

"Okay." He continued to stare at her, into the eyes that were glazed with shock. "Hang on. Don't try to be brave. Scream as much as you want but try not to move. I'll be quick." Bending further, he kissed her hard. "I promise."

Kate nodded, then concentrating on the feeling of his lips against hers, shut her eyes. He was quick. Within seconds she felt the hurt rip through her, over the threshold she thought she could bear and beyond.... She pulled in air to scream, but went back under the surface into liquid dimness.

Ky let the blood flow freely onto the deck for a moment, knowing it would wash away some of the poison. His hands had been rock steady when he'd pulled the spine from her flesh. His mind had been cold. Now with her blood on his hands, they began to shake. Ignoring them, and the icy fear of seeing Kate's smooth skin ripped and raw, Ky washed the wound, cleansed it, bound it. Within the hour, he'd have her to a doctor.

With unsteady fingers, he checked the pulse at the base of her neck. It wasn't strong, but it was steady. Lifting an eyelid with his thumb, he checked her pupils. He didn't believe she was in shock, she'd simply escaped from the pain. He thanked God for that.

On a long breath he let his forehead rest against hers, only for a moment. He prayed that she'd remain unconscious until she was safely under a doctor's care.

He didn't take the time to wash her blood from his hands before he took the helm. Ky whipped the boat around in a quick circle and headed full throttle back to Ocracoke.

# Chapter Seven

As she started to float toward consciousness, Kate focused, drifted, then focused again. She saw the whirl of a white ceiling rather than the pure blue arc of sky. Even when the mist returned she remembered the hurt and thrashed out against it. She couldn't face it a second time. Yet she found as she rose closer to the surface that she didn't have the will to fight against it. That brought fear. If she'd had the strength, she might have wept.

Then she felt a cool hand on her cheek. Ky's voice pierced the last layers of fog, low and gentle. "Take it easy, Kate. You're all right now. It's all over."

Though her breath hitched as she inhaled, Kate opened her eyes. The pain didn't come. All she felt was his hand on her cheek, all she saw was his face. "Ky." When she said his name, Kate reached for his hand, the one solid thing she was sure of. Her own voice frightened her. It was hardly more than a wisp of air.

"You're going to be fine. The doctor took care of you." As he spoke, Ky rubbed his thumb over her knuckles, establishing a point of concentration, and kept his other hand lightly on her cheek, knowing that contact was important. He'd nearly gone mad waiting for her to open her eyes again. "Dr. Bailey, you remember. You met him before."

It seemed vital that she should remember so she forced her mind to search back. She had a vague picture of a tough, weathered old man who looked more suited to the sea than the examining room. "Yes. He likes . . . likes ale and flounder."

He might have laughed at her memory if her voice had been stronger. "You're going to be fine, but he wants you to rest for a few more days."

"I feel . . . strange." She lifted a hand to her own head as if to assure herself it was still there.

"You're on medication, that's why you're groggy. Understand?"

"Yes." Slowly she turned her head and focused on her surroundings. The walls were a warm ivory, not the sterile white of a hospital. The dark oak trim gleamed dully. On the hardwood floor lay a single rug, its muted Indian design fading with age. It was the only thing Kate recognized. The last time she'd been in Ky's bedroom only half the dry wall had been in place and one of the windows had had a long thin crack in the bottom pane. "Not the hospital," she managed.

"No." He stroked her head, needing to touch as much as to check for her fever that had finally broken near dawn. "It was easier to bring you here after Bailey took care of you. You didn't need a hospital, but neither of us liked the idea of your being in a hotel right now."

"Your house," she murmured, struggling to concentrate her strength. "This is your bedroom, I remember the rug."

They'd made love on it once. That's what Ky remembered. With an effort, he kept his hands light. "Are you hungry?"

"I don't know." Basically, she felt nothing. When she tried to sit up, the drug spun in her head, making both the room and reality reel away. That would have to stop, Kate decided while she waited for the dizziness to pass. She'd rather have some pain than that helpless, weighted sensation.

Without fuss, Ky moved the pillows and shifted her to a sitting position. "The doctor said you should eat when you woke up. Just some soup." Rising he looked down on her, in much the same way, Kate thought, as he'd looked at a cracked mast he was considering mending. "I'll fix it. Don't get up," he added as he walked to the door. "You're not strong enough yet."

As he went into the hall he began to swear in a low steady stream.

Of course she wasn't strong enough, he thought with a last vicious curse. She was pale enough to fade into the sheets she lay on. No resistance, that's what Bailey had said. Not enough food, not enough sleep, too much strain. If he could do nothing else, Ky determined as he pulled open a kitchen cupboard, he could do something about that. She was going to eat, and lie flat on her back until the doctor said otherwise.

He'd known she was weak, that was the worst of it. Ky dumped the contents of a can into a pot then hurled the empty container into the trash. He'd seen the strain on her face, the shadows under her eyes, he'd heard the traces of fatigue come and go in her voice, but he'd been too wrapped up in his own needs to do anything about it.

With a flick of the wrist, he turned on the burner under the soup, then the burner under the coffee. God, he needed coffee. For a moment he simply stood with his fingers pressed against his eyes waiting for his system to settle.

He couldn't remember ever spending a more frantic twenty-four hours. Even after the doctor had checked and treated her, even when Ky had brought her home and she'd been fathoms deep under the drug, his nerves hadn't eased. He'd been terrified to leave the room for more than five minutes at a time. The fever had raged through her, though she'd been unaware. Most of the night he'd sat beside her, bathing away the sweat and talking to her, though she couldn't hear.

Through the night he'd existed on coffee and nerves. With a half-laugh he reached for a cup. It looked like that wasn't going to change for awhile yet.

He knew he still wanted her, knew he still felt something for her, under the bitterness and anger. But until he'd seen her lying unconscious on the deck of his boat, with her blood on his hands, he hadn't realized that he still loved her.

He'd known what to do about the want, even the bitterness, but now, faced with love, Ky hadn't a clue. It didn't seem possible for him to love someone so frail, so calm, so... different than he. Yet the emotion he'd once felt for her had grown and ripened into something so solid he couldn't see any way around it. For now, he'd concentrate on getting her on her feet again. He poured the soup into a bowl and carried it upstairs.

It would have been an easy matter to close her eyes and slide under again. Too easy. Willing herself to stay awake, Kate concentrated on Ky's room. There were a number of changes here as well, she mused. He'd trimmed the windows in oak, giving them a wide sill where he'd scattered the best of his shells. A piece of satiny driftwood stood, beautiful as a piece of sculpture. There was a paneled closet door with a faceted glass knob where there'd once been a rod, a round-backed rattan chair where there'd been packing crates.

Only the bed was the same, she mused. The wide four-poster had been his mother's. She knew he'd given the rest of his family's furniture to Marsh. Ky had told her once he'd felt no need or desire for it, but he kept the bed. He was born there, unexpectedly, during a night in which the island had been wracked by a storm.

And they'd made love there, Kate remembered as she ran her fingers over the sheets. The first time, and the last.

Stopping the movement of her fingers, she looked over as Ky came back into the room. Memories had to be pushed aside. "You've done a lot of work in here."

"A bit." He set the tray over her lap as he sat on the edge of the bed.

As the scent of the soup reached her, Kate shut her eyes. Just the aroma seemed to be enough. "It smells wonderful."

"The smell won't put any meat on you."

She smiled, and opened her eyes again. Then before she'd realized it, Ky had spoon-fed her the first bite. "It tastes wonderful too." Though she reached for the spoon, he dipped it into the bowl himself then held it to her lips. "I can do it," she began, then was forced to swallow more broth.

"Just eat." Fighting off waves of emotion he spoke briskly. "You look like hell."

"I'm sure I do," she said easily. "Most people don't look their best a couple of hours after being stung by a stingray."

"Twenty-four," Ky corrected as he fed her another spoon of soup.

"Twenty-four what?"

"Hours." Ky slipped in another spoonful when her eyes widened.

"I've been unconscious for twenty-four hours?" She looked to the window and the sunlight as if she could find some means of disproving it.

"You slipped in and out quite a bit before Bailey gave you the shot. He said you probably wouldn't remember." Thank God, Ky added silently. Whenever she'd fought her way back to consciousness, she'd been in agony. He could still hear her moans, feel the way she'd clutched him. He never knew a person could suffer physically for another's pain the way he'd suffered for hers. Even now it made his muscles clench.

"That must've been some shot he gave me."

"He gave you what you needed." His eyes met hers. For the first time Kate saw the fatigue in them, and the anger.

"You've been up all night," she murmured. "Haven't you had any rest at all?"

"You needed to be watched," he said briefly. "Bailey wanted you to stay under, so you'd sleep through the worst of the pain, and so you'd just sleep period." His voice changed as he lost control over the anger. He couldn't prevent the edge of accusation from showing, partly for her, partly for himself. "The wound wasn't that bad, do you understand? But you weren't in any shape to handle it. Bailey said you've been well on the way to working yourself into exhaustion."

"That's ridiculous. I don't—"

Ky swore at her, filling her mouth with more soup. "Don't tell me it's ridiculous. I had to listen to him. I had to look at you. You don't eat, you don't sleep, you're going to fall down on your face."

There was too much of the drug in her system to allow her temper to bite. Instead of annoyance, her words came out like a sigh. "I didn't fall on my face."

"Only a matter of time." Fury was coming too quickly. Though his fingers tightened on the spoon, Ky held it back. "I don't care how much you want to find the treasure, you can't enjoy it if you're flat on your back."

The soup was warming her. As much as her pride urged her to refuse, her system craved the food. "I won't be," she told him, not even aware that her words were beginning to slur. "We'll dive again tomorrow, and I'll prove it's the *Liberty*."

He started to swear at her, but one look at the heavy eyes and the pale cheeks had him swallowing the words. "Sure." He spooned in more soup knowing she'd be asleep again within moments.

"I'll give the ladle and the rigging and the rest to a museum." Her eyes closed. "For my father."

Ky set the tray on the floor. "Yes, I know."

"It was important to him. I need . . . I just need to give him something." Her eyes fluttered open briefly. "I didn't know he was ill. He never told me about his heart, about the pills. If I'd known . . ."

"You couldn't have done any more than you did." His voice was gentle again as he shifted the pillows down.

"I loved him."

"I know you did."

"I could never seem to make the people I love understand what I need. I don't know why."

"Rest now. When you're well, we'll find the treasure."

She felt herself sinking into warmth, softness, the dark. "Ky." Kate reached out and felt his fingers wrap around hers. With her eyes closed, it was all the reality she needed.

"I'll stay," he murmured, brushing the hair from her cheek. "Just rest."

"All those years..." He could feel her fingers relaxing in his as she slipped deeper. "I never forgot you. I never stopped wanting you. Not ever..."

He stared down at her as she slept. Her face was utterly peaceful, pale as marble, soft as silk. Unable to resist, he lifted her fingers to his own cheek, just to feel her flesh against his. He wouldn't think about what she'd said now. He couldn't. The strain of the last day had taken a toll on him as well. If he didn't get some rest, he wouldn't be able to care for her when she woke again.

Rising, Ky pulled down the shades, and took off his shirt. Then he lay down next to Kate in the big fourposter bed and slept for the first time in thirty-six hours.

The pain was a dull, consistent throb, not the silvery sharp flash she remembered, but a gnawing ache that wouldn't pass. When it woke her, Kate lay still, trying to orient herself. Her mind was clearer now. She was grateful for that, even though with the drug out of her system she was well aware of the wound. It was dark, but the moonlight slipped around the edges of the shades Ky had drawn. She was grateful for that too. It seemed she'd been a prisoner of the dark for too long.

It was night. She prayed it was only hours after she'd last awoken, not another full day later. She didn't want that quick panic at the thought of losing time again. Because she needed to be certain she was in control this time, she went over everything she remembered.

The pottery bowl, the ladle, then the stingray. She closed her eyes a moment, knowing it would be a very long time before she forgot what it had felt like to be struck with that whiplike tail. She remembered waking up on the deck of the *Vortex*, the pure blue sky overhead, and the strong, calm way Ky had spoken to her before he'd pulled out the spine. That pain, the horror of that one instant was very clear. Then, there was nothing else.

She remembered nothing of the journey back to the island, or of Dr. Bailey's ministrations or of being transported to Ky's home. Her next clear image was of waking in his bedroom, of dark oak trim on the windows, wide sills with shells set on them.

He'd fed her soup—yes, that was clear, but then things started to become hazy again. She knew he'd been angry, though she couldn't remember why. At the moment, it was more important to her that she could put events in some sort of sequence.

As she lay in the dark, fully awake and finally aware, she heard the sound of quiet, steady breathing beside her. Turning her head, Kate saw Ky beside her, hardly more than a silhouette with the moonlight just touching the skin of his chest so that she could see it rise and fall.

He'd said he would stay, she remembered. And he'd been tired. Abruptly Kate remembered there'd been fatigue in his eyes as well as temper. He'd been caring for her.

A mellow warmth moved through her, one she hadn't felt in a very long time. He had taken care of her, and though it had made him angry, he'd done it. And he'd stayed. Reaching out, she touched his cheek.

Though the gesture was whisper light, Ky awoke immediately. His sleep had been little more than a half doze so that he could recharge his system yet be aware of any sign that Kate needed attention. Sitting up, he shook his head to clear it.

He looked like a boy caught napping. For some reason the gesture moved Kate unbearably. "I didn't mean to wake you," she murmured.

He reached for the lamp beside the bed and turned it on low. Though his body revolted against the interruption, his mind was fully awake. "Pain?"

"No."

He studied her face carefully. The glazed look from the drug had left her eyes, but the color hadn't returned. "Kate."

"All right. Some."

"Bailey left some pills."

As he started to rise, Kate reached for him again. "No, I don't want anything. It makes me groggy."

"It takes away the pain."

"Not now, Ky, please. I promise I'll tell you if it gets bad."

Because her voice was close to desperate he made himself content with that. At the moment, she looked too fragile to argue with. "Are you hungry?"

She smiled, shaking her head. "No. It must be the middle of the night. I was only trying to orient myself." She touched him again, in gratitude, in comfort. "You should sleep."

"I've had enough. Anyway, you're the patient."

Automatically, he put his hand to her forehead to check for fever. Touched, Kate laid hers over it. She felt the quick reflexive tensing of his fingers.

"Thank you." When he would have removed his hand, she linked her fingers with his. "You've been taking good care of me."

"You needed it," he said simply and much too swiftly. He couldn't allow her to stir him now, not when they were in that big, soft bed surrounded by memories.

"You haven't left me since it happened."

"I had no place to go."

His answer made her smile. Kate reached up her free hand to touch his cheek. There had been changes, she thought, many changes. But so many things had stayed the same. "You were angry with me."

"You haven't been taking care of yourself." He told himself he should move away from the bed, from Kate, from everything that weakened him there.

He stayed, leaning over her, one hand caught in hers. Her eyes were dark, soft in the dim light, full of the sweetness and innocence he remembered. He wanted to hold her until there was no more pain for either of them, but he knew, if he pressed his body against hers now, he wouldn't stop. Again he started to move, pulling away the hand that held hers. Again Kate stopped him.

"I would've died if you hadn't gotten me up."

"That's why it's smarter to dive with a partner."

"I might still have died if you hadn't done everything you did."

He shrugged this off, too aware that the fingers on his face were stroking lightly, something she had done in the past. Sometimes before they'd made love, and often afterward, when they'd talked in quiet voices, she'd stroke his face, tracing the shape of it as though she'd needed to memorize it. Perhaps she, too, sometimes awoke in the middle of the night and remembered too much.

Unable to bear it, Ky put his hand around her wrist and drew it away. "The wound wasn't that bad," he said simply.

"I've never seen a stingray that large." She shivered and his hand tightened on her wrist.

"Don't think about it now. It's over."

Was it? she wondered as she lifted her head and looked into his eyes. Was anything ever really over? For four years she'd told herself there were joys and pains that could be forgotten, absorbed into the routine that was life as it had to be lived. Now, she was no longer sure. She needed to be. More than anything else, she needed to be sure.

"Hold me," she murmured.

Was she trying to make him crazy? Ky wondered. Did she want him to cross the border, that edge he was trying so desperately to avoid? It took most of the strength he had left just to keep his voice even. "Kate, you need to sleep now. In the morning—"

"I don't want to think about the morning," she murmured. "Only now. And now I need you to hold me." Before he could refuse, she slipped her arms around his waist and rested her head on his shoulder.

She felt his hesitation, but not his one vivid flash of longing before his arms came around her. On a long breath Kate closed her eyes. Too much time had passed since she'd had this, the gentleness, the sweetness she'd experienced only with Ky. No one else had ever held her with such kindness, such simple compassion. Somehow, she never found it odd that a man could be so reckless and arrogant, yet kind and compassionate at the same time.

Perhaps she'd been attracted to the recklessness, but it had been the kindness she had fallen in love with. Until now, in the quiet of the deep night, she hadn't understood. Until now, in the security of his arms, she hadn't accepted what she wanted.

Life as it had to be lived, she thought again. Was taking what she so desperately needed part of that?

She was so slender, so soft beneath the thin nightshirt. Her hair lay over his skin, loose and free, its color muted in the dim light. He could feel her palms against his back, those elegant hands that had always made him think more of an artist than a teacher. Her breathing was quiet, serene, as he knew it was when she slept. The light scent of woman clung to the material of the nightshirt.

Holding her didn't bring the pain he'd expected but a contentment he'd been aching for without realizing it. The tension in his muscles eased, the knot in his stomach vanished. With his eyes closed, he rested his cheek on her hair. It seemed like a lifetime since he'd known the pleasure of quiet satisfaction. She'd asked him to hold her, but had she known he needed to be held just as badly?

Kate felt him relax degree by degree and wondered if it had been she who'd caused the tension in him, and she who'd ultimately released it. Had she hurt him more than she'd realized? Had he cared more than she'd dared to believe? Or was it simply that the physical need never completely faded? It didn't matter, not tonight.

Ky was right. She knew the rules this time around. She wouldn't expect more than he offered. Whatever he offered was much, much more than she'd had in the long, dry years without him. In turn, she could give what she ached to give. Her love.

"It's the same for me as it always was," she murmured. Then, tilting her head back, she looked at him. Her hair streamed down her back, her eyes were wide and honest. He felt the need slam into him like a fist.

"Kate—"

"I never expected to feel the same way when I came back," she interrupted. "I don't think I'd have come. I wouldn't have had the courage."

"Kate, you're not well." He said it very slowly, as if he had to explain to them both. "You've lost blood, had a fever. It's taken a lot out of you. It'd be best, I think, if you tried to sleep now."

She felt no fever now. She felt cool and light and full of needs. "That day on the beach during the storm, you said I'd come to you." Kate brought her hands up his back until they reached his shoulders. "Even then I knew you were right. I'm coming to you now. Make love with me, Ky, here, in the bed where you loved me that first time."

And the last, he remembered, fighting back a torrent of desire. "You're not well," he managed a second time.

"Well enough to know what I want." She brushed her lips over his chin where his beard grew rough with neglect. So long... that was all that would come clearly to her. It had been so long. Too long. "Well enough to know what I need. It's always been you." Her fingers tightened on his shoulders, her lips inches from his. "It's only been you."

Perhaps moving away from her was the answer. But some answers were impossible. "Tomorrow you may be sorry."

She smiled in her calm, quiet way that always moved him. "Then we'll have tonight."

He couldn't resist her. The warmth. He didn't want to hurt her. The softness. The need building inside him threatened to send them both raging even though he knew she was still weak, still fragile. He remembered how it had been the first time, when she'd been innocent. He'd been so careful, though he had never felt the need to care before, and hadn't since. Remembering that, he laid her back.

"We'll have tonight," he repeated and touched his lips to hers.

Sweet, fresh, clean. Those words went through his head, those sensations went through his system as her lips parted for his. So he lingered over her kiss, enjoying with tenderness what he'd once promised himself to take ruthlessly. His mouth caressed, without haste, without pressure. Tasting, just tasting, while the hunger grew.

Her hands reached for his face, fingers stroking, the rough, the smooth. She could hear her own heart beat in her head, feel the slow, easy pleasure that came in liquid waves. He murmured to her, lovely, quiet words that made her thrill when she felt them formed against her mouth. With his tongue he teased hers in long, lazy sweeps until she felt her mind cloud as it had under the drug. Then when she felt the first twinge of desperation, he kissed her with an absorbed patience that left her weak.

He felt it—that initial change from equality to submission that had always excited him. The aggression would come later, knocking the breath from him, taking him to the edge. He knew that too. But for the moment, she was soft, yielding.

He slid his hands over the nightshirt, stroking, lingering. The material between his flesh and hers teased them both. She moved to his rhythm, glorying in the steady loss of control. He took her deeper with a touch, still deeper with a taste. She dove, knowing the full pleasure of ultimate trust. Wherever he took her, she wanted to go.

With a whispering movement he took his hand over the slender curve of her breast. She was soft, the material smooth, making her hardening nipple a sensuous contrast. He loitered there while her breathing grew unsteady, reveling in the changes of her body. Lingering over each separate button of her nightshirt, Ky unfastened them, then slowly parted the material, as if he were unveiling a priceless treasure.

He'd never forgotten how lovely she was, how exciting delicacy could be. Now that he had her again, he allowed himself the time to look, to touch carefully, all the while watching the contact of his lean tanned hand against her pale skin. With tenderness he felt seldom and demonstrated rarely, he lowered his mouth, letting his lips follow the progress his fingers had already begun.

She was coming to life under him. Kate felt her blood begin to boil as though it had lain dormant in her veins for years. She felt her heart begin to thump as though it had been frozen in ice until that moment. She heard her name as only he said it. As only he could.

Sensations? Could there be so many of them? Could she have known them all once, experienced them all once, then lived without them? A whisper, a sigh, the brush of a fingertip along her skin. The scent of a man touched by the sea, the taste of her lover lingering yet on her lips. The glow of soft lights against closed lids. Time faded. No yesterday. No tomorrow.

She could feel the slick material of the nightshirt slide away, then the warm, smooth sheets beneath her back. The skim of his tongue along her ribcage incited a thrill that began in her core and exploded inside her head.

She remembered the dawn breaking slowly over the sea. Now she knew the same magnificence inside her own body. Light and warmth spread through her, gradually, patiently, until she was glowing with a new beginning.

He hadn't known he could hold such raging desire in check and still feel such complete pleasure, such whirling excitement. He was aware of every heightening degree of passion that worked through her. He understood the changing, rippling thrill she felt if he used more pressure here, a longer taste there. It brought him a wild sense of power, made only more acute by the knowledge that he must harness it. She was fluid. She was silk. And then with a suddenness that sent him reeling, she was fire.

Her body arched on the first tumultuous crest. It ripped through her like a madness. Greedy, ravenous for more, she began to demand what he'd only hinted at. Her hands ran over him, nearly destroying his control in a matter of seconds. Her mouth was hot, hungry, and sought his with an urgency he couldn't resist. Then she rained kisses over his face, down his throat until he gripped the sheets with his hands for fear of crushing her too tightly and bruising her skin.

She touched him with those slender, elegant fingers so that the blood rushed fast and furious into his head. "You make me crazy," he murmured.

"Yes." She could do no more than whisper, but her eyes opened. "Yes."

"I want to watch you go up," he said softly as he slid into her. "I want to see what making love with me does to you."

She arched again, the moan inching out of her as she experienced a second wild peak. He saw her eyes darken, cloud as he took her slowly, steadily toward the verge between passion and madness. He watched the color come into her cheeks, saw her lips tremble as she spoke his name. Her hands gripped his shoulders, but neither of them knew her short tapered nails dug into his skin.

They moved together, neither able to lead, both able to follow. As pleasure built, he never took his eyes from her face.

All sensation focused into one. They were only one. With a freedom that reaches perfection only rarely, they gave perfection to each other.

# Chapter Eight

She was sleeping soundly when Ky woke. Ky observed a hint of color in her cheeks and was determined to see that it stayed there. The touch of his hand to her hair was gentle but proprietary. Her skin was cool and dry, her breathing quiet but steady.

What she'd given him the night before had been offered with complete freedom, without shadows of the past, with none of the bitter taste of regret. It was something else he intended to keep constant.

No, he wasn't going to allow her to withdraw from him again. Not an inch. He'd lost her four years ago, or perhaps he'd never really had her—not in the way he'd believed, not in the way he'd taken for granted. But this time, Ky determined, it would be different.

In his own way, he needed to take care of her. Her fragility drew that from him. In another way, he needed a partner on equal terms. Her strength offered him that. For reasons he never completely understood, Kate was exactly what he'd always wanted.

Clumsiness, arrogance, inexperience, or perhaps a combination of all three made him lose her once. Now that he had a second chance, he was going to make sure it worked. With a little more time, he might figure out how.

Rising, he dressed in the shaded light of the bedroom, then left her to sleep.

When she woke slowly, Kate was reluctant to surface from the simple pleasure of a dream. The room was dim, her mind was hazy with sleep and fantasy. The throb in her leg came as a surprise. How could there be pain when everything was so perfect? With a sigh, she reached for Ky and found the bed empty.

The haze vanished immediately, as did all traces of sleep and the pretty edge of fantasy. Kate sat up, and though the movement jolted the pain in her leg, she stared at the empty space beside her.

Had that been a dream as well? she wondered. Tentatively, she reached out and found the sheets cool. All a fantasy brought on by medication and confusion? Unsure, unsteady, she pushed the hair away from her face. Was it possible that she'd imagined it all—the gentleness, the sweetness, the passion?

She'd needed Ky. That hadn't been a dream. Even now she could feel the dull ache in her stomach that came from need. Had the need caused her to fantasize all that strange, stirring beauty during the night? The bed beside her was empty, the sheets cool. She was alone.

The pleasure she awoke with drained, leaving her empty, leaving her grateful for the pain that was her only grip on reality. She wanted to weep, but found she hadn't the energy for tears.

"So you're up."

Ky's voice made her whip her head around. Her nerves were strung tight. He walked into the bedroom carrying a tray, wearing an easy smile.

"That saves me from having to wake you up to get some food into you." Before he approached the bed, he went to both windows and drew up the shades. Light poured into the room and the warm breeze that had been trapped behind the shades rushed in to ruffle the sheets.

Feeling it, she had to control a shudder. "How'd you sleep?"

"Fine." The awkwardness was unexpected. Kate folded her hands and sat perfectly still. "I want to thank you for everything you've done."

"You've already thanked me once. It wasn't necessary then or now." Because her tone had put him on guard, Ky stopped next to the bed to take a good long look at her. "You're hurting."

"It's not bad."

"This time you take a pill." After setting the tray on her lap, he walked to the dresser and picked up a small bottle. "No arguments," he said, anticipating her refusal.

"Ky, it's really not bad." When had he offered her a pill before? The struggle to remember brought only more frustration. "There's barely any pain."

"Any pain's too much." He sat on the bed, and putting the pill into her palm curled her hand over it with his own. "When it's you."

With her fingers curled warmly under his, she knew. Elation came so quietly she was afraid to move and chase it away. "I didn't dream it, did I?" she whispered.

"Dream what?" He kissed the back of her hand before he handed her the glass of juice.

"Last night. When I woke up, I was afraid it had all been a dream."

He smiled and, bending, touched his lips to hers. "If it was, I had the same dream." He kissed her again, with humor in his eyes. "It was wonderful."

"Then it doesn't matter whether it was a dream or not."

"Oh no, I prefer reality."

With a laugh, she started to drop the pill on the tray, but he stopped her. "Ky—"

"You're hurting," he said again. "I can see it in your eyes. Your medication wore off hours ago, Kate."

"And kept me unconscious for an entire day."

"This is mild, just to take the edge off. Listen—" His hand tightened on hers. "I had to watch you in agony."

"Ky, don't."

"No, you'll do it for me if not for yourself. I had to watch you bleed and faint and drift in and out of consciousness." He ran his hand down her hair, then cupped her face so she'd look directly into his eyes. "I can't tell you what it did to me because I don't know how to describe it. I know I can't watch you in pain any more."

In silence, she took the pill and drained the glass of juice. For him, as he said, not for herself. When she swallowed the medication, Ky tugged at her hair. "It hardly has more punch than an aspirin, Kate. Bailey said he'd give you something stronger if you needed it, but he'd rather you go with this."

"It'll be fine. It's really more uncomfortable than painful." It wasn't quite the truth, nor did he believe her, but they both let it lie for the moment. Each of them moved cautiously, afraid to spoil what might have begun to bloom again. Kate glanced down at the empty juice glass. The cold, fresh flavor still lingered on her tongue. "Did Dr. Bailey say when I could dive again?"

"Dive?" Ky's brows rose as he uncovered the plate of bacon, eggs and toast. "Kate, you're not even getting up out of bed for the rest of the week."

"Out of bed?" she repeated. "A week?" She ignored the overloaded plate of food as she gaped at him. "Ky, I was stung by a stingray, not attacked by a shark."

"You were stung by a stingray," he agreed. "And your system was so depleted Bailey almost sent you to a hospital. I realize things might've been rough on you since your father died, but you haven't helped anything by not taking care of yourself."

It was the first time he'd mentioned her father's death, and Kate noted he still expressed no sympathy. "Doctors tend to fuss," she began.

"Bailey doesn't," he interrupted. The anger came back and ran along the edge of his words. "He's a tough, cynical old goat, but he knows his business. He told me that you'd apparently worked yourself right to the edge of exhaustion, that your resistance was nil, and that you were a good ten pounds underweight." He held out the fork. "We're going to do something about that, professor. Starting now."

Kate looked down at what had to be four large eggs, scrambled, six slices of bacon and four pieces of toast. "I can see you intend to," she murmured.

"I'm not having you sick." He took her hand again and his grip was firm. "I'm going to take care of you, Kate, whether you like it or not."

She looked back at him in her calm, considering way. "I don't know if I do like it," she decided. "But I suppose we'll both find out."

Ky dipped the fork into the eggs. "Eat."

A smile played at the corners of her mouth. She'd never been pampered in her life and thought it might be entirely too easy to get used to it. "All right, but this time I'll feed myself."

She already knew she'd never finish the entire meal, but for his sake, and the sake of peace, she determined to deal with half of it. That had been precisely his strategy. If he'd have brought her a smaller portion, she'd have eaten half of that, and have eaten less. He knew her better than either one of them fully realized.

"You're still a wonderful cook," she commented, breaking a piece of bacon in half. "Much better than I."

"If you're good, I might broil up some flounder tonight."

She remembered just how exquisitely he prepared fish. "How good?"

"As good as it takes." He accepted the slice of toast she offered him but dumped on a generous slab of jam. "Maybe I'll beg some of the hot fudge cake from the Roost."

"Looks like I'll have to be on my best behavior."

"That's the idea."

"Ky..." She was already beginning to poke at her eggs. Had eating always been quite such an effort? "About last night, what happened—"

"Should never have stopped," he finished.

Her lashes swept up, and her eyes were quiet and candid. "I'm not sure."

"I am," he countered. Taking her face in his hands, he kissed her, softly, with only a hint of passion. But the hint was a promise of much more. "Let it be enough for now, Kate. If it has to get complicated, let's wait until other things are a little more settled."

Complicated. Were commitments complicated, the future, promises? She looked down at her plate knowing she simply didn't have the strength to ask or to answer. Not now. "In a way I feel as though I'm slipping back—to that summer four years ago. And yet..."

"It's like a step forward."

Kate looked at him again, but this time reached out. He'd always understood. Though he said little, though his way was sometimes rough, he'd always understood. "Yes. Either way it's a little unnerving."

"I've never liked smooth water. You get a better ride with a few waves."

"Perhaps." She shook her head. Slipping back, stepping forward, it hardly mattered. Either way, she was moving toward him. "Ky, I can't eat any more."

"I figured." Easily, he picked up an extra fork from the tray and began eating the cooling eggs himself. "It's still probably more than you eat for breakfast in a week."

"Probably," she agreed in a murmur, realizing just how well he'd maneuvered her. Kate lay back against the propped-up pillows, annoyed that she was growing sleepy again. No more medication, she decided silently as Ky polished off their joint breakfast. If she could just avoid that, and go out for a little while, she'd be fine. The trick would be to convince Ky.

Kate looked toward the window, and the sunshine. "I don't want to lose a week's time going over the wreck."

He didn't have to follow the direction of her gaze to follow the direction of her thoughts. "I'll be going down," he said easily. "Tomorrow, the next day anyway." Sooner, he thought to himself, depending on how Kate mended.

"Alone?"

He caught the tone as he bit into the last piece of bacon. "I've gone down alone before."

She would have protested, stating how dangerous it was, if she'd believed it would have done any good. Ky did a great deal alone because that was how he preferred it. Instead, Kate chose another route.

"We're looking for the *Liberty* together, Ky. It isn't a one-man operation."

He sent her a long, quiet look before he picked up the coffee she hadn't touched. "Afraid I'll take off with the treasure?"

"Of course not." She wouldn't allow her emotions to get in the way. "If I hadn't trusted your integrity," she said evenly, "I wouldn't have shown you the chart in the first place."

"Fair enough," he allowed with a nod. "So if I continue to dive while you're recuperating, we won't lose time."

"I don't want to lose you either." It was out before she could stop it. Swearing lightly, Kate looked toward the window again. The sky was the pale blue sometimes seen on summer mornings.

Ky merely sat for a moment while the pleasure of her words rippled through him. "You'd worry about me?"

Angry, Kate turned back. He looked so smug, so infuriatingly content. "No, I wouldn't worry. God usually makes a point of looking after fools."

Grinning, he set the tray on the floor beside the bed. "Maybe I'd like you to worry, a little."

"Sorry I can't oblige you."

"Your voice gets very prim when you're annoyed," he commented. "I like it."

"I'm not prim."

He ran a hand down her loosened hair. No, she looked anything but prim at the moment. Soft and feminine, but not prim. "Your voice is. Like one of those pretty, lacy ladies who used to sit in parlors eating finger sandwiches."

She pushed his hand aside. He wouldn't get around her with charm. "Perhaps I should shout instead."

"Like that too, but more..." He kissed one cheek, then the other. "I like to see you smile at me. The way you smile at nobody else."

Her skin was already beginning to warm. No, he might not get around her with charm, but... he'd distract her from her point if she wasn't careful. "I'd be bored, that's all. If I have to sit here, hour after hour with nothing to do."

"I've got lots of books." He slipped her nightshirt down her shoulder then kissed her bare skin with the lightest of touches. "Probably lay my hands on some crossword puzzles, too."

"Thanks a lot."

"There's a copy of Byron downstairs."

Despite her determination not to, Kate looked toward him again. "Byron?"

"I bought it after you left. The words are wonderful." He had the three buttons undone with such quick expertise, she never noticed. "But I could always hear the way you'd say them. I remember one night on the beach, when the moon was full on the water. I don't remember the name of the poem, but I remember how it started, and how it sounded when you said it. 'It is the hour'," he began, then smiled at her.

"'It is the hour'," Kate continued, "'when from the boughs the nightingale is heard/It is the hour when lovers' vows seem sweet in every whisper'd word/And gentle winds, and waters near make music to the lonely ear'..." She trailed off, remembering even the scent of that night. "You were never very interested in Byron's technique."

"No matter how hard you tried to explain it to me."

Yes, he was distracting her. Kate was already finding it difficult to remember what point she'd been trying to make. "He was one of the leading poets of his day."

"Hmm." Ky caught the lobe of her ear between his teeth.

"He had a fascination for war and conflict, and yet he had more love affairs in his poems than Shelley or Keats."

"How about out of his poems?"

"There too." She closed her eyes as his tongue began to do outrageous things to her nervous system. "He used humor, satire as well as a pure lyrical style. If he'd ever completed *Don Juan* . . ." She trailed off with a sigh that edged toward a moan.

"Did I interrupt you?" Ky brushed his fingers down her thigh. "I really love to hear you lecture."

"Yes."

"Good." He traced her lips with his tongue. "I just thought maybe I could give you something to do for awhile." He skimmed his hand over her hip then up to the side of her breast. "So you won't be bored by staying in bed. Want to tell me more about Byron?"

With a long quiet breath, she wound her arms around his neck. The point she'd been trying to make didn't seem important any longer. "No, but I might like staying in bed after all, even without the crossword puzzles."

"You'll relax." He said it softly, but the command was unmistakable. She might have argued, but the kiss was long and lingering, leaving her slow and helplessly yielding.

"I don't have a choice," she murmured. "Between the medication and you."

"That's the idea." He'd love her, Ky thought, but so gently she'd have nothing to do but feel. Then she'd sleep.

"There are things I want from you." He lifted his head until their eyes met. "Things I need from you."

"You never tell me what they are."

"Maybe not." He laid his forehead on hers. Maybe he just didn't know how to tell her. Or how to ask. "For now, what I want is to see you well." Again he lifted his head, and his eyes focused on hers. "I'm not an unselfish man, Kate. I want that just as much for myself as I want it for you. I fully intended to have you back in my bed, but I didn't want it for you. I fully intended to have you back in my bed, but I didn't care to have you unconscious here first."

"Whatever you intended, I make my own choices." Her hands slid up his shoulders to touch his face. "I chose to make love with you then. I choose to make love with you now."

He laughed and pressed her palm to his lips. "Professor, you think I'd have given you a choice? Maybe we don't know each other as well as we should at this point, but you should know that much."

Thoughtfully, she ran her thumb down his cheekbone. It was hard, elegantly defined. Somehow it suited him in the same way the unshaven face suited him. But did she? Kate wondered. Were they, despite all their differences, right for each other?

It seemed when they were like this, there was no question of suitability, no question of what was right or wrong. Each completed the other. Yet there had to be more. No matter how much each of them denied it on the surface, there had to be more. And ultimately, there had to be a choice.

"When you take what isn't offered freely, you have nothing." She felt the rough scrape of his unshaven face on her palm and the thrill went through her system. "If I give, you have whatever you need without asking."

"Do I?" he murmured before he touched his lips to hers again. "And you? What do you have?"

She closed her eyes as her body drifted on a calm, quiet plane of pleasure. "What I need."

For how long? The question ran through his mind, prodding against his contentment. But he didn't ask. There'd be a time, he knew, for more questions, for the hundreds of demands he wanted to make. For ultimatums. Now she was sleepy, relaxed in the way he wanted her to be.

With no more words he let her body drift, stroking gently, letting her system steep in the pleasure he could give. With no one else could he remember asking so little for himself and receiving so much. She was the hinge that could open or close the door on the better part of him.

He listened to her sigh as he touched her. The second was a kind of pure contentment that mirrored his own feelings. It seemed neither of them required any more.

Kate knew it shouldn't be so simple. It had never been simple with anyone else, so that in the end she'd never given herself to anyone else. Only with Ky had she ever known that full excitement that left her free. Only with Ky had she ever known the pure ease that felt so right.

They'd been apart four years, yet if it had been forty, she would have recognized his touch in an instant. That touch was all she needed to make her want him.

She remembered the demands and fire that had always been threaded through their lovemaking before. It had been the excitement she'd craved even while it had baffled her. Now there was patience touched with a consideration she didn't know he was capable of.

Perhaps if she hadn't loved him already, she would have fallen in love at that moment when the sun filtered through the windows and his hands were on her skin. She wanted to give him the fire, but his hands kept it banked. She wanted to meet any demands, but he made none. Instead, she floated on the clouds he brought to her.

Though the heat smoldered inside him, she kept him sane. Just by her pliancy. Though passion began to take over, she kept him calm. Just by her serenity. He'd never looked for serenity in his life. It had simply come to him, as Kate had. He'd never understood what it meant to be calm, but he had known the emptiness and the chaos of living without it.

Without urgency or force, he slipped inside her. Slowly, with a sweetness that made her weak, he gave her the ultimate gift. Passion, fulfillment, with the softer emotions covering a need that seemed insatiable.

Then she slept, and he left her to her dreams.

When she awoke again, Kate wasn't groggy, but weak. Even as sleep cleared, a sense of helpless annoyance went though her. It was midafternoon. She didn't need a clock, the angle of the sunlight that slanted through the window across from the bed told her what time it was. More hours had been lost without her knowledge. And where was Ky?

Kate groped for her nightshirt and slipped into it. If he followed his pattern, he'd be popping through the door with a loaded lunch tray and a pill. Not this time, Kate determined as she eased herself out of bed. Nothing else was going into her system that made her lose time.

But as she stood, the dregs of the medication swam in her head. Reflexively, she nearly sat again before she stopped herself. Infuriated, she gripped the bedpost, breathed deeply then put her weight on her injured foot. It took the pain to clear her head.

Pain had its uses, she thought grimly. After she'd given the hurt a moment to subside, it eased into a throb. That could be tolerated, she told herself and walked to the mirror over Ky's dresser.

She didn't like what she saw. Her hair was listless, her face washed-out and her eyes dull. Swearing, she put her hands to her cheeks and rubbed as though she could force color into them. What she needed, Kate decided, was a hot shower, a shampoo and some fresh air. Regardless of what Ky thought, she was going to have them.

Taking a deep breath, she headed for the door. Even as she reached for the knob, it opened.

"What're you doing up?"

Though they were precisely the words she'd expected, Kate had expected them from Ky, not Linda. "I was just—"

"Do you want Ky to skin me alive?" Linda demanded, backing Kate toward the bed with a tray of steaming soup in her hand. "Listen, you're supposed to rest and eat, then eat and rest. Orders."

Realizing abruptly that she was retreating, Kate held her ground. "Whose?"

"Ky's. And," she continued before Kate could retort. "Dr. Bailey's."

"I don't have to take orders from either of them."

"Maybe you don't," Linda agreed dryly. "But I don't argue with a man who's protecting his woman, or with the man who poked a needle into my bottom when I was three. Both of them can be nasty. Now lie down."

"Linda . . ." Though she knew the sigh sounded long suffering, Kate couldn't prevent it. "I've a cut on my leg. I've been in bed for something like forty-eight hours straight. If I don't have a shower and a breath of air soon, I'm going to go crazy.''

A smile tugged at Linda's mouth that she partially concealed by nibbling on her lower lip. "A bit grumpy, are we?"

"I can be more than a bit." This time the sigh was simply bad tempered. "Look at me!" Kate demanded, tugging on her hair. "I feel as though I've just crawled out from under a rock."

"Okay. I know how I felt after I'd delivered Hope. After I'd had my cuddle with her I wanted a shower and shampoo so bad I was close to tears." She set the tray on the table beside the bed. "You can have ten minutes in the shower, then you can eat while I change your bandage. But Ky made me swear I'd make you eat every bite." She put her hands on her hips. "So that's the deal."

"He's overreacting," Kate began. "It's absurd. I don't need to be babied this way."

"Tell me that when you don't look like I could blow you over. Now come on, I'll give you a hand in the shower."

"No, dammit, I'm perfectly capable of taking a shower by myself." Ignoring the pain in her leg, she stormed out of the room, slamming the door at her back. Linda swallowed a laugh and sat down on the bed to wait.

Fifteen minutes later, refreshed and thoroughly ashamed of herself, Kate came back in. Wrapped in Ky's robe, she rubbed a towel over her hair. "Linda—"

"Don't apologize. If I'd been stuck in bed for two days, I'd snap at the first person who gave me trouble. Besides—" Linda knew how to play her cards "—if you're really sorry you'll eat all your soup, so Ky won't yell at me."

"All right." Resigned, Kate sat back in the bed and took the tray on her lap. She swallowed the first bite of soup and stifled her objection as Linda began to fiddle with her bandage. "It's wonderful."

"The seafood chowder's one of our specialties. Oh, honey." Linda's eyes darkened with concern after she removed the gauze. "This must've hurt like hell. No wonder Ky's been frantic."

Drumming up her courage, Kate leaned over enough to look at the wound. There was no inflammation as she'd feared, no puffiness. Though the slice was six inches in length, it was clean. Her stomach muscles unknotted. "It's not so bad," she murmured. "There's no infection."

"Look, I've been caught by a stingray, a small one. I probably had a cut half an inch across and I cried like a baby. Don't tell me it's not so bad."

"Well, I slept through most of it." She winced, then deliberately relaxed her muscles.

Linda narrowed her eyes as she studied Kate's face. "Ky said you should have a pill if there was any pain when you woke."

"If you want to do me a favor, you can dump them out." Calmly, Kate ate another spoonful of soup. "I really hate to argue with him, or with you, but I'm not taking any more pills and losing any more time. I appreciate the fact that he wants to pamper me. It's unexpectedly sweet, but I can only take it so far."

"He's worried about you. He feels responsible."

"For my carelessness?" With a shake of her head, Kate concentrated on finishing the soup. "It was an accident, and if there's blame, it's mine. I was so wrapped up in looking for salvage I didn't take basic precautions. I practically bumped into the ray." With an effort, she controlled a shudder. "Ky acted much more quickly than I. He'd already started to pull me out of range. If he hadn't, things would have been much more serious."

"He loves you."

Kate's fingers tightened on the spoon. With exaggerated care, she set it back on the tray. "Linda, there's a vast difference between concern, attraction, even affection and love."

Linda simply nodded in agreement. "Yes. I said Ky loves you."

She managed to smile and pick up the tea that had been cooling beside the soup. "*You* said," Kate returned simply. "*Ky* hasn't."

"Well neither did Marsh until I was ready to strangle him, but that didn't stop me."

"I'm not you." Kate lay back against the pillows, grateful that most of the weakness and the weariness had passed. "And Ky isn't Marsh."

Impatient, Linda rose and swirled around the room. "People who complicate simple things make me so mad!"

Smiling, Kate sipped her tea. "Others simplify the complicated."

With a sniff, Linda turned back. "I've known Ky Silver all my life. I watched him bounce around from one cute girl to the next, then one attractive woman to another until I lost count. Then you came along." Stopping, she leaned against the bedpost. "It was as if someone had hit him over the head with a blunt instrument. You dazed him, Kate, almost from the first minute. You fascinated him."

"Dazing, fascinating." Kate shrugged while she tried to ignore the ache in her heart. "Flattering, I suppose, but neither of those things equals love."

The stubborn line came and went between Linda's brows. "I don't believe love comes in an instant, it grows. If you could have seen the way Ky was after you left four years ago, you'd know—"

"Don't tell me about four years ago," Kate interrupted. "What happened four years ago is over. Ky and I are two different people today, with different expectations. This time..." She took a deep breath. "This time when it ends, I won't be hurt because I know the limits."

"You've just gotten back together and you're already talking about endings and limitations!" Dragging a hand through her hair, Linda came forward to sit on the edge of the bed. "What's wrong with you? Don't you know how to wish anymore? How to dream?"

"I was never very good at either. Linda..." She hesitated, wanting to choose her phrasing carefully. "I don't want to expect any more from Ky than what he can easily give. After August, I know we'll each go back to our separate worlds—there's no bridge between them. Maybe I was meant to come back so we could make up for whatever pain we caused each other before. This time I want to leave still being friends. He's..." She hesitated again because this phrasing was even more important. "He's always been a very important part of my life."

Linda waited a moment, then narrowed her eyes. "That's about the dumbest thing I've ever heard."

Despite herself, Kate laughed. "Linda—"

Holding up her hands, she shook her head and cut Kate off. "No, I can't talk about it anymore, I get too mad and I'm supposed to be taking care of you." She let out her breath on a huff as she removed Kate's tray. "I just can't understand how anyone so smart could be so stupid, but the more I think about it the more I can see that you and Ky deserve each other."

"That sounds more like an insult than a compliment."

"It was."

Kate pushed her tongue against her teeth to hold back a smile. "I see."

"Don't look so smug just because you've made me so angry I don't want to talk about it anymore." She drew her shoulders back. "I might just give Ky a piece of my mind when he gets home."

"That's his problem," Kate said cheerfully. "Where'd he go?"

"Diving."

Amusement faded. "Alone?"

"There's no use worrying about it." Linda spoke briskly as she cursed herself for not thinking of a simple lie. "He dives alone ninety percent of the time."

"I know." But Kate folded her hands, preparing to worry until he returned.

# Chapter Nine

"I'm going with you."

The sunlight was strong, the scent of the ocean pure. Through the screen the sound of gulls from a quarter of a mile away could be heard clearly. Ky turned from the stove where he poured the last cup of coffee and eyed Kate as she stood in the doorway.

She'd pinned her hair up and had dressed in thin cotton pants and a shirt, both of which were baggy and cool. It occured to him that she looked more like a student than a college professor.

He knew enough of women and their illusions to see that she'd added color to her cheeks. She hadn't needed blusher the evening before when he'd returned from the wreck. Then she had been angry, and passionate. He nearly smiled as he lifted his cup.

"You wasted your time getting dressed," he said easily. "You're going back to bed."

Kate disliked stubborn people, people who demanded their own way flatly and unreasonably. At that moment, she decided they were *both* stubborn. "No." On the surface she remained as calm as he was while she walked into the kitchen. "I'm going with you."

Unlike Kate, Ky never minded a good argument. Preparing for one, he leaned back against the stove. "I don't take down a diver against doctor's orders."

She'd expected that. With a shrug, she opened the refrigerator and took out a bottle of juice. She knew she was being bad tempered, and though it was completely out of character, she was enjoying the experience. The simple truth was that she had to do something or go mad.

As far as she could remember, she'd never spent two more listless days. She had to move, think, feel the sun. It might have been satisfying to stomp her feet and demand, but, she thought, fruitless. If she had to compromise to get her way, then compromise she would.

"I can rent a boat and equipment and go down on my own." With the glass in hand, she turned, challenging. "You can't stop me."

"Try me."

It was said simply, quietly, but she'd seen the flare of anger in his eyes. Better, she thought. Much better. "I've a right to do precisely as I choose. We both know it." Perhaps her leg was uncomfortable, but as to the rest of her body, it was charged up and ready to move. Nor was there anything wrong with her mind. Kate had plotted her strategy very well. After all, she thought grimly, there'd certainly been enough time to think it through.

"We both know you're not in any shape to dive." His first urge was to carry her back to bed, his second to shake her until she rattled. Ky did neither, only drank his coffee and watched her over the rim. A power struggle wasn't something he'd expected, but he wouldn't back away from it. "You're not stupid Kate. You know you can't go down yet, and you know I won't let you."

"I've rested for two days. I feel fine." As she walked toward him she was pleased to see him frown. He understood she had a mind of her own, and that he had to deal with it. The truth was, she was stronger than either of them had expected her to be. "As far as diving goes, I'm willing to leave that to you for the next couple of days, but..." She paused, wanting to be certain he knew she was negotiating, not conceding. "I'm going out on the *Vortex* with you. And I'm going out this morning."

He lifted a brow. She'd never intended to dive, but she'd used it as a pressure point to get what she wanted. He couldn't blame her. Ky remembered recovering from a broken leg when he was fourteen. The pain was vague in his mind now, but the boredom was still perfectly clear. "You'll lie down in the cabin when you're told."

She smiled and shook her head. "I'll lie down in the cabin if I need to."

He took her chin in his hand and squeezed. "Damn right you will. Okay, let's go. I want an early start."

Once he was resigned, Ky moved quickly. She could either keep up, or be left behind. Within minutes he parked his car near his slip at Silver Lake Harbor and was boarding the *Vortex*. Content, Kate took a seat beside him at the helm and prepared to enjoy the sun and the wind. Already she felt the energy begin to churn.

"I've done a chart of the wreck as of yesterday's dive," he told her as he maneuvered out of the harbor.

"A chart?" Automatically she pushed at her hair as she turned toward him. "You didn't show me."

"Because you were asleep when I finished it."

"I've been asleep ninety percent of the time," she mumbled.

As he headed out to sea, Ky laid a hand on her shoulder. "You look better Kate, no shadows. No strain. That's more important."

For a moment, just a moment, she pressed her cheek against his hand. Few women could resist such soft concern, and yet...she didn't want his concern to cloud their reason for being together. Concern could turn to pity. She needed him to see her as a partner, as equal. As long as she was his lover, it was vital that they meet on the same ground. Then when she left ... When she left there'd be no regrets.

"I don't need to be pampered anymore, Ky."

His shoulders moved as he glanced at the compass. "I enjoyed it."

She was resisting being cared for. He understood it, appreciated it and regretted it. There had been something appealing about seeing to her needs, about having her depend on him. He didn't know how to tell her he wanted her to be well and strong just as much as he wanted her to turn to him in times of need.

Somehow, he felt their time together had been too short for him to speak. He didn't deal well with caution. As a diver, he knew its importance, but as a man ... As a man he fretted to go with his instincts, with his impulses.

His fingers brushed her neck briefly before he turned to the wheel. He'd already decided he'd have to approach his relationship with Kate as he'd approach a very deep, very dangerous dive—with an eye on currents, pressure and the unexpected.

"That chart's in the cabin," he told her as he cut the engine. "You might want to look it over while I'm down."

She agreed with a nod, but the restlessness was already on her as Ky began to don his equipment. She didn't want to make an issue of his diving alone. He wouldn't listen to her in any case; if anything came of it, it would only be an argument. In silence she watched him check his tanks. He'd be down for an hour. Kate was already marking time.

"There are cold drinks in the galley." He adjusted the strap of his mask before climbing over the side. "Don't sit in the sun too long."

"Be careful," she blurted out before she could stop herself.

Ky grinned, then was gone with a quiet splash.

Though she ran over to the side, Kate was too late to watch him dive. For a long time after, she simply leaned over the boat, staring at the water's surface. She imagined Ky going deeper, deeper, adjusting his pressure, moving out with power until he'd reached the bottom and the wreck.

He'd brought back the bowl and ladle the evening before. They sat on the dresser in his bedroom while the broken rigging and pieces of crockery were stored downstairs. Thus far he'd done no more than gather what they'd already found together, but today, Kate thought with a twinge of impatience, he'd extend the search. Whatever he found, he'd find alone.

She turned away from the water, frustrated that she was excluded. It occurred to her that all her life she'd been an onlooker, someone who analyzed and explained the action rather than causing it. This search had been her first opportunity to change that, and now she was back to square one.

Stuffing her hands in her pockets, Kate looked up at the sky. There were clouds to the west, but they were thin and white. Harmless. She felt too much like that herself at the moment—something unsubstantial. Sighing, she went below deck. There was nothing to do now but wait.

Ky found two more cannons and sent up buoys to mark their position. It would be possible, if he didn't find something more concrete, to salvage the cannons and have them dated by an expert. Though he swam from end to end, searching carefully, he knew it was unlikely he'd find a date stamp through the layers of corrosion. But in time... Satisfied, he swam north.

If he accomplished nothing else on this dive, he wanted to establish the size of the site. With luck it would be fairly small, perhaps no bigger than a football field. However, there was always the chance that the wreckage could be scattered over several square miles. Before they brought in a salvage ship, he wanted to take a great deal of care with the preliminary work.

They would need tools. A metal detector would be invaluable. Thus far, they'd done no more than find a wreck, no matter how certain Kate was that it was the *Liberty*. For the moment he had no way to determine the origin of the ship, he had to find cargo. Once he'd found that, perhaps treasure would follow.

Once he'd found the treasure... Would she leave? Would she take her share of the gold and the artifacts and drive home?

Not if he could help it, Ky determined as he shone his headlamp over the sea floor. When the search was over and they'd salvaged what could be salvaged from the sea, it would be time to salvage what they'd once had—what had perhaps never truly been lost. If they could find what had been buried for centuries, they could find what had been buried for four years.

He couldn't find much without tools. Most of the ship—or what remained of it—was buried under silt. On another dive, he'd use the prop-wash, the excavation device he'd constructed in his shop. With that he could blow away inches of sediment at a time—a slow but safe way to uncover artifacts. But someone would have to stay on board to run it.

He thought of Kate and rejected the idea immediately. Though he had no doubt she could handle the technical aspect—it would only have to be explained to her once—she'd never go for it. Ky began to think it was time they enlisted Marsh.

He knew his air time was almost up and he'd have to surface for fresh tanks. Still, he lingered near the bottom, searching, prodding. He wanted to take something up for Kate, something tangible that would put the enthusiasm back in her eyes.

It took him more than half of his allotted time to find it, but when Ky held the unbroken bottle in his hand, he knew Kate's reaction would be worth the effort. It was a common bottle, not priceless crystal, but he could see no mold marks, which meant it had been hand blown. Crust was weathered over it in layers, but Ky took the time to carefully chip some away, from the bottom only. If the date wasn't on the bottom, he'd need the crust to have the bottle dated. Already he was thinking of the Corning Glass Museum and their rate of success.

Then he saw the date, and with a satisfied grin placed the find in the goodie bag on his belt. With his air supply running short, he started toward the surface.

His hour was up. Or so nearly up, Kate thought, that he should have surfaced already if he'd allowed himself any safety factor. She paced from port to starboard and back again. Would he always risk his own welfare to the limit?

She'd long since given up sitting quietly in the cabin, going over the makeshift chart Ky had begun. She'd found a book on shipwrecks that Ky had obviously purchased recently, and though it had also been among her father's research books, she'd skimmed through it again.

It gave a detailed guide to identifying and excavating a wreck, listed common mistakes and hazards. She found it difficult to read about hazards while Ky was alone beneath the surface. Still, even the simple language of the book couldn't disguise the adventure. For perhaps half the time Ky had been gone, she'd lost herself in it. Spanish galleons, Dutch merchant ships, English frigates.

She'd found the list of wrecks off North Carolina alone extensive. But these, she'd thought, had already been located, documented. The adventure there was over. One day, because of the chain her father had started and she'd continued, the *Liberty* would be among them.

Fretfully, Kate waited for Ky to surface. She thought of her father. He'd pored over this same book as well—planning, calculating. Yet his calculations hadn't taken him beyond the initial stage. If he'd shared his goal with her, would he have taken her on his summer quests? She'd never know, because she'd never been given the choice.

She was making her own choices now, Kate mused. Her first had been to return to Ocracoke, accepting the consequences. Her next had been to give herself to Ky without conditions. Her last, she thought as she stared down at the quiet water, would be to leave him again. Yet, in reality, perhaps she'd still been given no choice. It was all a matter of currents. She could only swim against them for so long.

Relief washed over her when she spotted the flow of bubbles. Ky grabbed the bottom rung of the ladder as he pushed up his mask. "Waiting for me?"

Relief mixed with annoyance for the time she'd spent worrying about him. "You cut it close."

"Yeah, a little." He passed up his tanks. "I had to stop and get you a present."

"It's not a joke, Ky." Kate watched him come over the side, agile, lean and energetic. "You'd be furious with me if I'd cut my time that close."

"Leave it up to Linda to fuss," he advised as he pulled down the zipper of his wet suit. "She was born that way." Then he grabbed her, crushing her against him so that she felt the excitement he'd brought up with him. His mouth closed over hers, tasting of salt from the sea. Because he was wet, her clothes clung to him, binding them together for the brief instant he held her. But when he would have released her, she held fast, drawing the kiss out into something that warmed his cool skin.

"I worry about you, Ky." For one last moment, she held on fiercely. "Damn it, is that what you want to hear?"

"No." He took her face in his hands and shook his head. "No."

Kate broke away, afraid she'd say too much, afraid she'd say things neither of them were ready to hear. She knew the rules this time. She groped for something calm, something simple. "I suppose I got a bit frantic waiting up here. It's different when you're down."

"Yeah." What did she want from him, he wondered? Why was it that every time she started to show her concern for him, she clammed up? "I've got some more things to add to the chart."

"I saw the buoys you sent up." Kate moistened her lips and relaxed, muscle by muscle.

"Two more cannons. From the size of them, I'd say she was a fairly small ship. It's unlikely she was constructed for battle."

"She was a merchant ship."

"Maybe. I'm going to take the metal detector down and see what I come up with. From the stuff we've found, I don't think she's buried too deep."

Kate nodded. Delve into business, keep the personal aspect light. "I'd like to send off a piece of the planking and some of the glass to be analyzed. I think we'll have more luck with the glass, but it doesn't hurt to cover all the angles."

"No, it doesn't. Don't you want your present?"

At ease again, she smiled. "I thought you were joking. Did you bring me a shell?"

"I thought you'd like this better." Reaching into his bag, Ky brought out the bottle. "It's too bad it's not still corked. We could've had wine with peanut butter."

"Oh, Ky, it's not damaged!" Thrilled, she reached out for it, but he pulled it back out of reach and grinned.

"Bottoms up," he told her and turned the bottle upside down.

Kate stared at the smeared bottom of the bottle. "Oh, God," she whispered. "It's dated. 1749." Gingerly, she took the bottle in both hands. "The year before the *Liberty* sank."

"It's another ship, maybe," Ky reminded her. "But it does narrow down the time element."

"Over two hundred years," she murmured. "Glass, it's so breakable, so vulnerable, and yet it survived two centuries." Her eyes lit with enthusiasm as she looked back at him. "Ky, we should be able to find out where the bottle was made."

"Probably, but most glass bottles found on wrecks from the seventeenth and eighteenth century were manufactured in England anyway. It wouldn't prove the ship was English."

She let out a huff of breath, but her energy hadn't dimmed. "You've been doing your research."

"I don't go into any project until I know the angles." Ky knelt down to check the fresh tanks.

"You're going back down now?"

"I want to get as much mapped out as I can before we start dealing with too much equipment."

She'd done enough homework herself to know that the most common mistake of the modern day salvor was in failing to map out a site. Yet she couldn't stem her impatience. It seemed so time-consuming when they could be concentrating on getting under the layers of silt.

It seemed to her that she and Ky had changed positions somehow. She'd always been the cautious one, proceeding step by logical step, while he'd taken the risks. Struggling with the impotence of having to wait and watch, she stood back while he strapped on the fresh tanks. As she watched, Ky picked up a brass rod.

"What's that for?"

"It's the base for this." He held out a device that resembled a compass. "It's called an azimuth circle. It's a cheap, effective way to map out the site. I drive this into the approximate center of the wreck so that it becomes the datum point, align the circle with the magnetic north, then I use a length of chain to measure the distance to the cannons, or whatever I need to map. After I get it set, I'll be back up for the metal detector."

Frustration built again. He was doing all the work while she simply stood still. "Ky, I feel fine. I could help if—"

"No." He didn't bother to argue or list reasons. He simply went over the side and under.

It was midafternoon when they started back. Ky spent the last hour at sea adding to the chart, putting in the information he'd gathered that day. He'd brought more up in his goodie bag—a tankard, spoons and forks that might have been made of iron. It seemed they had indeed found the galley. Kate decided she'd begin a detailed list of their finds that evening. If it was all she could do at the moment, she'd do it with pleasure.

Her mood had lifted a bit since she'd caught three good-sized bluefish while Ky had been down at the wreck the second time. No matter how much Ky argued, she fully intended to cook them herself and eat them sitting at the table, not lying in bed.

"Pretty pleased with yourself aren't you?"

She gave him a cool smile. They were cruising back toward Silver Lake harbor and though she felt a weariness, it was a pleasant feeling, not the dragging fatigue of the past days. "Three bluefish in that amount of time's a very respectable haul."

"No argument there. Especially since I intend to eat half of them."

"I'm going to grill them."

"Are you?"

She met his lifted brow with a neutral look. "I caught, I cook."

Ky kept the boat at an even speed as he studied her. She looked a bit tired, but he thought he could convince her to take a nap if he claimed he wanted one himself. She was healing quickly. And she was right. He couldn't pamper her. "I could probably bring myself to start the charcoal for you."

"Fair enough. I'll even let you clean them."

He laughed at the bland tone and ruffled her hair until the pins fell out.

"Ky!" Automatically, Kate reached up to repair the damage.

"Wear it up in the school room," he advised, tossing some of the pins overboard. "I find it difficult to resist you when your hair's down and just a bit mussed."

"Is that so?" She debated being annoyed, then decided there were more productive ways to pass the time. Kate let the wind toss her hair as she moved closer to him so that their bodies touched. She smiled at the quick look of surprise in his eyes as she slipped both hands under his T-shirt. "Why don't you turn off the engine and show me what happens when you stop resisting?"

For all her generosity and freedom in lovemaking, she'd never been the initiator. Ky found himself both baffled and aroused as she smiled up at him, her hands stroking slowly over his chest. "You know what happens when I stop resisting," he murmured.

She gave a low, quiet laugh. "Refresh my memory." Without waiting for an answer, she drew back on the throttle herself until the boat was simply idling. "You didn't make love with me last night." Her hands slid around and up his back.

"You were sleeping." She was seducing him in the middle of the afternoon, in the middle of the ocean. He found he wanted to savor the new experience as much as he wanted to bring it to fruition.

"I'm not sleeping now." Rising on her toes, she brushed her lips over his, lightly, temptingly. She felt his heartbeat race against her body and reveled in a sense of power she'd never explored. "Or perhaps you're in a hurry to get back, and uh, clean fish."

She was taunting him. Why had he never seen the witch in her before? Ky felt his stomach knot with need, but when he drew her closer, she resisted. Just slightly. Just enough to torment. "If I make love with you now, I won't be gentle."

She kept her lips inches from his. "Is that a warning?" she whispered. "Or a promise?"

He felt the first tremor move through him and was astonished. Not even for her had he ever trembled. Not even for her. The need grew, stretching restlessly, recklessly. "I'm not sure you know what you're doing, Kate."

Nor did she, but she smiled because it no longer mattered. Only the outcome mattered. "Come down to the cabin with me and we'll both find out." She slipped away from him and without a word disappeared below deck.

His hand wasn't steady when he reached for the key to turn off the engines. He needed a moment, perhaps a bit more, to regain the control he'd held so carefully since they'd become lovers again. Even since he'd had her blood on his hands, he had a tremendous fear of hurting her. Since he'd had a taste of her again, he had an equal fear of driving her away. Caution was a strain, but he'd kept it in focus with sheer will. As Ky started down the steps, he told himself he'd continue to be cautious.

She'd unbuttoned her blouse but hadn't removed it. When he came into the narrow cabin with her, Kate smiled. She was afraid, though she hardly knew why. But over the fear was a heady sense of power and strength that fought for full release. She wanted to take him to the edge, to push him to the limits of passion. At that moment, she was certain she could.

When he came no closer to her, Kate stepped forward and pulled his shirt over his head. "Your skin's gold," she murmured. "It's always excited me." Taking her pleasure slowly, she ran her hands up his sides, feeling the quiver she caused. "You've always excited me."

Her hands were steady, her pulse throbbed as she unsnapped his cut-offs. With her eyes on his, she slowly,

slowly, undressed him. "No one's ever made me want the way you make me want."

He had to stop her and take control again. She couldn't know the effect of those long, fragile fingers when they brushed easily over his skin, or how her calm eyes made him rage inside.

"Kate..." He took her hands in his and bent to kiss her. But she turned her head, meeting his neck with warm lips that sent a spear of fire up his spine.

Then her body was pressed against his, flesh meeting flesh where her blouse parted. Her mouth trailed over his chest, her hands down his back to his hips. He felt the fury of desire whip through him as though it had sharp, hungry teeth.

So he forgot control, gentleness, vulnerability. She drove him to forget. She intended to.

They were tangled on the narrow bunk, her blouse halfway down her back and parted so that her breasts pushed into his chest, driving him mad with their firm, subtle curves. She nipped at his lips, demanding, pushing for more, still more. Waves of passion overtook them.

His need was incendiary. She was like a flame, impossible to hold, searing here, singeing there until his body was burning with needs and fierce fantasies.

Her hands were swift, sending sharp gasping pleasure everywhere at once until he wasn't sure he could take it anymore. Yet he no longer thought of stopping her. Less of stopping himself.

His hands gripped her with an urgency that made her moan from the sheer strength in them. She wanted his strength now—mindless strength that would carry them both to a place they'd never gone before. And she was leading. The knowledge made her laugh aloud as she tasted his skin, his lips, his tongue.

She slid down his body, feeling each jolt of pleasure as it shot through him. There could be no slow, lingering loving now. They'd pushed each other beyond reason. The air here was dark and thin and whirling with sound. Kate drank it in.

When he found her moist, hot and ready she let him take her over peak after shuddering peak, knowing as he drove her, she drove him. Her body was filled with sensations that came and went like comets, slipped away and burst on her again, and again. Through the thunder in her head she heard herself say his name, clear and quick.

On the sound, she took him into her and welcomed the madness.

# Chapter Ten

She was wrong.

Kate had thought she'd be ready, even anxious to dive again. There hadn't been a day during her recuperation that she hadn't thought of going down. Every time Ky had brought back an artifact, she was thrilled with the discovery and frustrated with her own lack of participation. Like a schoolgirl approaching summer, she'd begun to count the days.

Now, a week after the accident, Kate stood on the deck of the *Vortex* with her mouth dry and her hands trembling as she pulled on her wet suit. She could only be grateful that Ky was already over the side, hooking up his home-rigged prop-wash to the boat's propeller. Drafted to the crew, Marsh stood at the stern watching his brother. With Linda's eager support, he'd agreed to give Ky a few hours a day of his precious free time while he was needed.

Kate took the moment she had alone to gather her thoughts and her nerve.

It was only natural to be anxious about diving after the experience she'd had. Kate told herself that was logical. But it didn't stop her hands from trembling as she zipped up her suit. She could equate it with falling off a horse and having to mount again. It was psychological. But it didn't ease the painful tension in her stomach.

Trembling hands and nerves. With or without them she told herself as she hooked on her weight belt, she was going down. Nothing, not even her own fears, was going to stop her from finishing what she'd begun.

"He's got it," Marsh called out when Ky signaled him.

"I'll be ready." Kate picked up the cloth bag she'd use to bring up small artifacts. With luck, and if the prop-wash did its job, she knew they'd soon need more sophisticated methods to bring up the salvage.

"Kate."

She didn't look up, but continued to hook on the goodie bag. "Yes?"

"You know it's only natural that you'd be nervous going down." Marsh touched a hand to her shoulder, but she busied herself by strapping on her diving knife. "If you want a little more time, I'll work with Ky and you can run the wash."

"No." She said it too quickly, then cursed herself. "It's all right, Marsh." With forced calm she hung the underwater camera she'd purchased only the day before around her neck. "I have to take the first dive sometime."

"It doesn't have to be now."

She smiled at him again thinking how calm, how steady he appeared when compared to Ky. This was the sort of man it would have made sense for her to be attracted to. Confused emotions made no sense. "Yes, it does. Please." She put her hand on his arm before he could speak again. "Don't say anything to Ky."

Did she think he'd have to, Marsh wondered as he inclined his head in agreement. Unless he was way off the mark, Marsh was certain Ky knew every expression, every gesture, every intonation of her voice.

"Let's run it a couple of minutes at full throttle." Ky climbed over the side, dripping and eager. "With the depth and the size of the prop, we're going to have to test the effect. There might not be enough power to do us any good."

In agreement, Marsh went to the helm. "Are you thinking about using an air lift?"

Ky's only answer was a noncommital grunt. He had thought of it. The metal tube with its stream of compressed air was a quick, efficient way to excavate on silty bottoms. They might get away with the use of a small air lift, if it became necessary. But perhaps the prop-wash would do the job well enough. Either way, he was thinking more seriously about a bigger ship, with more sophisticated equipment and more power. As he saw it, it all depended on what they found today.

He picked up one last piece of equipment—a small powerful spear gun. He'd take no more chances with Kate.

"Okay, slow it down to the minimum," he ordered. "And keep it there. Once Kate and I are down, we don't want the prop-wash shooting cannonballs around."

Kate stopped the deep breathing she was using to ease tension. Her voice was cool and steady. "Would it have that kind of power?"

"Not at this speed." Ky adjusted his mask then took her hand. "Ready?"

"Yes."

Then he kissed her, hard. "You've got guts, professor," he murmured. His eyes were dark, intense as they passed over her face. "It's one of the sexiest things about you." With this he was over the side.

He knew. Kate gave a quiet unsteady sigh as she started down the ladder. He knew she was afraid, and that had been his way of giving her support. She looked up once and saw Marsh. He lifted his hand in salute. Throat dry, nerves jumping, Kate let the sea take her.

She felt a moment's panic, a complete disorientation the moment she was submerged. It ran through her head that down here, she was helpless. The deeper she went, the more vulnerable she became. Choking for air, she kicked back toward the surface and the light.

Then Ky had her hands, holding her to him, holding her under. His grip was firm, stilling the first panic. Feeling the wild race of her pulse, he held on during her first resistance.

Then he touched her cheek, waiting until she'd calmed enough to look at him. In his eyes she saw strength and challenge. Pride alone forced her to fight her way beyond the fear and meet him, equal to equal.

When she'd regulated her breathing, accepting that her air came through the tanks on her back, he kissed the back of her hand. Kate felt the tension give. She wouldn't be helpless, she reminded herself. She'd be careful.

With a nod, she pointed down, indicating she was ready to dive. Keeping hands linked, they started toward the bottom.

The whirlpool action created by the wash of the prop had already blasted away some of the sediment. At first glance Ky could see that if the wreck was buried under more than a few feet, they'd need something stronger than his home-made apparatus and single prop engine. But for now, it would do. Patience, which came to him only with deliberate effort, was more important at this stage than speed. With the wreck, he thought, and—he glanced over at the woman beside him—with a great deal more. He had to take care not to hurry.

It was still working, blowing away some of the over-burden at a rate Ky figured would equal an inch per minute. He and Kate alone couldn't deal with any more speed. He watched the swirl of water and sediment while she swam a few feet away to catalog one of the cannons on film. When she came closer, he grinned as she placed the camera in front of her face again. She was relaxed, her initial fear forgotten. He could see it simply in the way she moved. Then she let the camera fall so they could begin the search again.

Kate saw something solid wash away from the hole being created by the whirl of water. Grabbing it up, she found herself holding a candlestick. In her excitement, she turned it over and over in her hand.

Silver? she wondered with a rush of adrenaline. Had they found their first real treasure? It was black with oxidation, so it was impossible to be certain what it was made of. Still, it thrilled her. After days and days of only waiting, she was again pursuing the dream.

When she looked up, Ky was already gathering the uncovered items and laying them in the mesh basket. There were more candleholders, more tableware, but not the plain unglazed pottery they'd found before. Kate's pulse began to drum with excitement while she meticulously snapped pictures. They'd be able to find a hallmark, she was certain of it. Then they'd know if they had indeed found a British ship. Ordinary seamen didn't use silver, or even pewter table service. They'd uncovered more than the galley now. And they were just beginning.

When Ky found the first piece of porcelain he signaled to her. True, the vase—if that's what it once had been—had suffered under the water pressure and the years. It was broken so that only half of the shell remained, but so did the manufacturer's mark.

When Kate read it, she gripped Ky's arm. *Whieldon.* English. The master potter who'd trained the likes of

Wedgwood. Kate cupped the broken fragment in her hands as though it were alive. When she lifted her eyes to Ky's they were filled with triumph.

Fretting against her inability to speak, Kate pointed to the mark again. Ky merely nodded and indicated the basket. Though she was loath to part with it, Kate found herself even more eager to discover more. She settled the porcelain in the mesh. When she swam back, Ky's hands were filled with other pieces. Some were hardly more than shards, others were identifiable as pieces left from bowls or lids.

No, it didn't prove it was a merchant ship, Kate told herself as she gathered what she could herself. So far, it only proved that the officers and perhaps some passengers had eaten elegantly on their way to the New World. English officers, she reminded herself. In her mind they'd taken the identification that far.

The force of the wash sent an object shooting up. Ky reached out for it and found a crusted, filthy pot he guessed would have been used for tea or coffee. Perhaps it was cracked under the layers, but it held together in his hands. He tapped on his tank to get Kate's attention.

She knew it was priceless the moment she saw it. Stemming impatience, she signaled for Ky to hold it out as she lifted the camera again. Obliging, he crossed his legs like a genie and posed.

It made her giggle. They'd perhaps just found something worth thousands of dollars, but he could still act silly. Nothing was too serious for Ky. As she brought him into frame, Kate felt the same foolish pleasure. She'd known the hunt would be exciting, perhaps rewarding, but she'd never known it would be fun. She swam forward and reached for the vase herself.

Running her fingers over it, she could detect some kind of design under the crust. Not ordinary pottery, she was sure. Not utility-ware. She held something elegant, something well crafted.

He understood its worth as well as she. Taking it from her, Ky indicated they would bring it and the rest of the morning's salvage to the surface. Pointing to his watch he showed her that their tanks were running low.

She didn't argue. They'd come back. The *Liberty* would wait for them. Each took a handle of the mesh basket and swam leisurely toward the surface.

"Do you know how I feel?" Kate demanded the moment she could speak.

"Yes." Ky gripped the ladder with one hand and waited for her to unstrap her tanks and slip them over onto the deck. "I know just how you feel."

"The teapot." Breathing fast, she hauled herself up the ladder. "Ky, it's priceless. It's like finding a perfectly formed rose inside a mass of briars." Before he could answer, she was laughing and calling out to Marsh. "It's fabulous! Absolutely fabulous."

Marsh cut the engine then walked over to help them. "You two work fast." Bending he touched a tentative finger to the pot. "God, it's all in one piece."

"We'll be able to date it as soon as it's cleaned. But look." Kate drew out the broken vase. "This is the mark of an English potter. English," she repeated, turning to Ky. "He trained Wedgwood, and Wedgwood didn't begin manufacturing until the 1760s, so—"

"So this piece more than likely came from the era we're looking for," Ky finished. "*Liberty* or not," he continued, crouching down beside her. "It looks like you've found yourself an eighteenth-century wreck that's probably of English origin and certainly hasn't been recorded before.'' He took one of her hands between both of his. ''Your father would've been proud of you.''

Stunned, she stared at him. Emotions raced through her with such velocity she had no way of controlling or channeling them. The hand holding the broken vase began to tremble. Quickly, she set it down in the basket again and rose.

''I'm going below,'' she managed and fled.

Proud of her. Kate put a hand over her mouth as she stumbled into the cabin. His pride, his love. Wasn't it all she'd really ever wanted from her father? Was it possible she could only gain it after his death?

She drank in deep gulps of air and struggled to level her emotions. No, she wanted to find the *Liberty*, she wanted to bring her father's dream to reality, have his name on a plaque in a museum with the artifacts they'd found. She owed him that. But she'd promised herself she'd find the *Liberty* for herself as well. For herself.

It was her choice, her first real decision to come in from the sidelines and act on her own. For herself, Kate thought again as she brought the first surge of emotion under control.

''Kate?''

She turned, and though she thought she was perfectly calm, Ky could see the turmoil in her eyes. Unsure how to handle it, he spoke practically.

''You'd better get out of that suit.''

''But we're going back down.''

''Not today.'' To prove his point he began to strip out of his own suit just as Marsh started the engines.

Automatically, she balanced herself as the boat turned. ''Ky, we've got two more sets of tanks. There's no reason for us to go back when we're just getting started.''

"Your first dive took most of the strength you've built up. If you want to dive tomorrow, you've got to take it slow today."

Her anger erupted so quickly, it left them both astonished. "The hell with that!" she exploded. "I'm sick to death of being treated as if I don't know my own limitations or my own mind and body."

Ky walked into the galley and picked up a can of beer. With a flick of his wrist, air hissed out. "I don't know what you're talking about."

"I lay in bed for the better part of a week because of pressure from you and Linda and anyone else who came around me. I'm not tolerating this any longer."

With one hand, he pushed dripping hair from his forehead as he lifted the can. "You're tolerating exactly what's necessary until I say differently."

"You say?" she tossed back. Cheeks flaming, she strode over to him. "I don't have to do what you say, or what anyone says. Not anymore. It's about time you remember just who's in charge of this salvage operation."

His eyes narrowed. "In charge?"

"I hired you. Seventy-five a day and twenty-five percent. Those were the terms. There was nothing in there about you running my life."

He abruptly went still. For a moment, all that could be heard over the engines was her angry breathing. Dollars and percents, he thought with a deadly sort of calm. Just dollars and percents. "So that's what it comes down to?"

Too overwrought to see beyond her own anger, she continued to lash out. "We made an agreement. I fully intend to see that you get everything we arranged, but I won't have you telling me when I can go down. I won't have you judging when I'm well and when I'm not. I'm sick to death of being dictated to. And I won't be—not by you, not by anyone. Not any longer."

The metal of the can gave under his fingers. "Fine. You do exactly what you want, professor. But while you're about it, get yourself another diver. I'll send you a bill." Ky went up the cabin steps the way he came down. Quickly and without a sound.

With her hands gripped together, Kate sat down on the bunk and waited until she heard the engines stop again. She refused to think. Thinking hurt. She refused to feel. There was too much to feel. When she was certain she was in control, she stood up and went up on deck.

Everything was exactly as she'd left it—the wire basket filled with bits of porcelain and tableware, her nearly depleted tanks. Ky was gone. Marsh walked over from the stern where he'd been waiting for her.

"You're going to need a hand with these."

Kate nodded and pulled a thigh length T-shirt over her tank suit. "Yes. I want to take everything back to my room at the hotel. I have to arrange for shipping."

"Okay." But instead of reaching down for the basket, he took her arm. "Kate, I don't like to give advice."

"Good." Then she swore at her own rudeness. "I'm sorry, Marsh. I'm feeling a little rough at the moment."

"I can see that, and I know things aren't always smooth for you and Ky. Look, he has a habit of closing himself up, of not saying everything that's on his mind. Or worse," Marsh added. "Of saying the first thing that comes to mind."

"He's perfectly free to do so. I came here for the specific purpose of finding and excavating the *Liberty*. If Ky and I can't deal together on a business level, I have to do without his help."

"Listen, he has a few blind spots."

"Marsh, you're his brother. Your allegiance is with him as it should be."

"I care about both of you."

She took a deep breath, refusing to let the emotion surface and carry her with it. "I appreciate that. The best thing you can do for me now, perhaps for both of us, is to tell me where I can rent a boat and some equipment. I'm going back out this afternoon."

"Kate."

"I'm going back out this afternoon," she repeated. "With or without your help."

Resigned, Marsh picked up the mesh basket. "All right, you can use mine."

It took the rest of the morning for Kate to arrange everything, including the resolution of a lengthy argument with Marsh. She refused to let him come with her, ending by saying she'd simply rent a boat and do without his assistance altogether. In the end, she stood at the helm of his boat alone and headed out to sea.

She craved the solitude. Almost in defiance, she pushed the throttle forward. If it was defiance, she didn't care, anymore than she cared whom she was defying. It was vital to do this one act for herself.

She refused to think about Ky, about why she'd exploded at him. If her words had been harsh, they'd also been necessary. She comforted herself with that. For too long, for a lifetime, she'd been influenced by someone else's opinion, someone else's expectations.

Mechanically, she stopped the engines and put on her equipment, checking and rechecking as she went. She'd never gone down alone before. Even that seemed suddenly a vital thing to do.

With a last look at her compass, she took the mesh basket over the side.

As she went deep, a thrill went through her. She was alone. In acres and acres of sea, she was alone. The water parted for her like silk. She was in control, and her destiny was her own.

She didn't rush. Kate found she wanted that euphoric feeling of being isolated under the sea where only curious fish bothered to give her a passing glance. Ultimately, her only responsibility here was to herself. Briefly, she closed her eyes and floated. At last, only to herself.

When she reached the site, she felt a new surge of pride. This was something she'd done without her father. She wouldn't think of the whys or the hows now, but simply the triumph. For two centuries, it had waited. And now, *she'd* found it. She circled the hole the propwash had created and began to fan using her hand.

Her first find was a dinner plate with a flamboyant floral pattern around the rim. She found one, then half a dozen, two of which were intact. On the back was the mark of an English potter. There were cups as well, dainty, exquisite English china that might have graced the table of a wealthy colonist, might have become a beloved heirloom, if nature hadn't interfered. Now they looked like something out of a horror show—crusted, misshapen with sea life. They couldn't have been more beautiful to her.

As she continued to fan, Kate nearly missed what appeared to be a dark sea shell. On closer examination she saw it was a silver coin. She couldn't make out the currency, but knew it didn't matter. It could just as easily be Spanish, as she'd read that Spanish currency had been used by all European nations with settlements in the New World.

The point was, it was a coin. The first coin. Though it was silver, not gold, and unidentifiable at the moment, she'd found it by herself.

Kate started to slip it into her goodie bag when her arm was jerked back.

The thrill of fear went wildly from her toes to her throat. The spear gun was on board the *Vortex*. She had no weapon. Before she could do more than turn in defense, she was caught by the shoulders with Ky's furious hands.

Terror died, but the anger in his eyes only incited her own. Damn him for frightening her, for interfering. Shaking him away, Kate signaled for him to leave. With one arm, he encircled her waist and started for the surface.

Only once did she even come close to breaking away from him. Ky simply banded his arm around her again, more tightly, until she had a choice between submitting or cutting off her own air.

When they broke the surface, Kate drew in breath to shout, but even in this, she was out-maneuvered.

"Idiot!" he shouted at her, dragging her to the ladder. "One day off your back and you jump into forty feet of water by yourself. I don't know why in hell I ever thought you had any brains."

Breathless, she heaved her tanks over the side. When she was on solid ground again, she intended to have her say. For now, she'd let him have his.

"I take my eyes off you for a couple hours and you go off half-cocked. If I'd murdered Marsh, it would have been on your head."

To her further fury, Kate saw that she'd boarded the *Vortex*. Marsh's boat was nowhere in sight.

"Where's the *Gull*?" she demanded.

"Marsh had the sense to tell me what you were doing." The words came out like bullets as he stripped his gear. "I didn't kill him because I needed him to come out with me and take the *Gull* back." He stood in front of her, dripping, and as furious as she'd ever seen him. "Don't you have any more sense than to dive out here alone?"

She tossed her head back. "Don't you?"

Infuriated, he grabbed her and started to peel the wet suit from her himself. "We're not talking about me, damn it. I've been diving since I was six. I know the currents."

"*I* know the currents."

"And I haven't been flat on my back for a week."

"I was flat on my back for a week because you were overreacting." She struggled away from him, and because the wet suit was already down to her waist, peeled it off. "You've no right to tell me when and where I can dive, Ky. Superior strength gives you no right to drag me up when I'm in the middle of salvaging."

"The hell with what I have a right to do." Grabbing her again, he shook her with more violence than he'd ever shown her. A dozen things might have happened to her in the thirty minutes she'd been down. A dozen things he knew too well. "I make my own rights. You're not going down alone if I have to chain you up to stop it."

"You told me to get another diver," she said between her teeth. "Until I do, I dive alone."

"You threw that damn business arrangement in my face. Percentages. Lousy percentages and a daily rate. Do you know how that made me feel?"

"No!" she shouted, pushing him away. "No, I don't know how that made you feel. I don't know how anything makes you feel. You don't tell me." Dragging both hands through her dripping hair she walked away. "We agreed to the terms. That's all I know."

"That was before."

"Before what?" she demanded. Tears brimmed for no reason she could name, but she blinked them back again. "Before I slept with you?"

"Damn it, Kate." He was across the deck, backing her into the rail before she could take a breath. "Are you trying to get at me for something I did or didn't do four years ago? I don't even know what it is. I don't know what you want from me or what you don't want and I'm sick of trying to outguess you."

"I don't want to be pushed into a corner," she told him fiercely. "That's what I don't want. I don't want to be expected to fall in passively with someone else's plans for me. That's what I don't want. I don't want it assumed that I simply don't have any personal goals or wishes of my own. Or any basic competence of my own. *That's* what I don't want!"

"Fine." They were both losing control, but he no longer gave a damn. Ky ripped off his wet suit and tossed it aside. "You just remember something, lady. I don't expect of you and I don't assume. Once maybe, but not anymore. There was only one person who ever pushed you into a corner and it wasn't me." He hurled his mask across the deck where it bounced and smacked into the side. "I'm the one who let you go."

She stiffened. Even with the distance between them he could see her eyes frost over. "I won't discuss my father with you."

"You caught on real quick though, didn't you?"

"You resented him. You—"

"I?" Ky interrupted. "Maybe you better look at yourself, Kate."

"I loved him," she said passionately. "All my life I tried to show him. You don't understand."

"How do you know that I don't understand?" he exploded. "Don't you know I can see what you're feeling every time we find something down there? Do you think I'm so blind I don't see that you're hurting because *you* found it, not him? Don't you think it tears me apart to see that you punish yourself for not being what you think he wanted you to be? And I'm tired," he continued as her breath started to hitch. "Damn tired of being compared to and measured by a man you loved without ever being close to him."

"I don't." She covered her face, hating the weakness but powerless against it. "I don't do that. I only want..."

"What?" he demanded. "What do you want?"

"I didn't cry when he died," she said into her hands. "I didn't cry, not even at the funeral. I owed him tears, Ky. I owed him something."

"You don't owe him anything you didn't already give him over and over again." Frustrated, he dragged a hand through his hair before he went to her. "Kate." Because words seemed useless, he simply gathered her close.

"I didn't cry."

"Cry now," he murmured. He pressed his lips to the top of her head. "Cry now."

So she did, desperately, for what she'd never been able to quite touch, for what she'd never been able to quite hold. She'd ached for love, for the simple companionship of understanding. She wept because it was too late for that now from her father. She wept because she wasn't certain she could ask for love again from anyone else.

Ky held her, lowering her onto the bench as he cradled her in his lap. He couldn't offer her words of comfort.

They were the most difficult words for him to come by. He could only offer her a place to weep, and silence.

As the tears began to pass, she kept her face against his shoulder. There was such simplicity there, though it came from a man of complications. Such gentleness, though it sprang from a restless nature. "I couldn't mourn for him before," she murmured. "I'm not sure why."

"You don't have to cry to mourn."

"Maybe not," she said wearily. "I don't know. But it's true, what you said. I've wanted to do all this for him because he'll never have the chance to finish what he started. I don't know if you can understand, but I feel if I do this I'll have done everything I could. For him, and for myself."

"Kate." Ky tipped back her head so he could see her face. Her eyes were puffy, rimmed with red. "I don't have to understand. I just have to love you."

He felt her stiffen in his arms and immediately cursed himself. Why was it he never said things to her the way they should be said? Sweetly, calmly, softly. She was a woman who needed soft words, and he was a man who always struggled with them.

She didn't move, and for a long, long moment, they stayed precisely as they were.

"Do you?" she managed after a moment.

"Do I what?"

Would he make her drag it from him? "Love me?"

"Kate." Frustrated, he drew away from her. "I don't know how else to show you. You want bouquets of flowers, bottles of French champagne, poems? Damn it, I'm not made that way."

"I want a straight answer."

He let out a short breath. Sometimes her very calmness drove him to distraction. "I've always loved you. I've never stopped."

That went through her, sharp, hot, with a mixture of pain and pleasure she wasn't quite sure how to deal with. Slowly, she rose out of his arms, and walking across the deck, looked out to sea. The buoys that marked the site bobbed gently. Why were there no buoys in life to show you the way?

"You never told me."

"Look, I can't even count the number of women I've said it to." When she turned back with her brow raised, he rose, uncomfortable. "It was easy to say it to them because it didn't mean anything. It's a hell of a lot harder to get the words out when you mean them, and when you're afraid someone's going to back away from you the minute you do."

"I wouldn't have done that."

"You backed away, you went away for four years, when I asked you to stay."

"You asked me to stay," she reminded him. "You asked me not to go back to Connecticut, but to move in with you. Just like that. No promises, no commitment, no sign that you had any intention of building a life with me. I had responsibilities."

"To do what your father wanted you to do."

She swallowed that. It was true in its way. "All right, yes. But you never said you loved me."

He came closer. "I'm telling you now."

She nodded, but her heart was in her throat. "And I'm not backing away. I'm just not sure I can take the next step. I'm not sure you can either."

"You want a promise."

She shook her head, not certain what she'd do if indeed he gave her one. "I want time, for both of us. It seems we both have a lot of thinking to do."

"Kate." Impatient, he came to her, taking her hands. They trembled. "Some things you don't have to think about. Some things you can think about too much."

"You've lived your life a certain way a long time, and I mine," she said quickly. "Ky, I've just begun to change—to feel the change. I don't want to make a mistake, not with you. It's too important. With time—"

"We've lost four years," he interrupted. He needed to resolve something, he discovered, and quickly. "I can't wait any longer to hear it if it's inside you."

Kate let out the breath she'd been holding. If he could ask, she could give. It would be enough. "I love you, Ky. I never stopped either. I never told you when I should have."

He felt the weight drain from his body as he cupped her face. "You're telling me now."

It was enough.

# Chapter Eleven

Love. Kate had read hundreds of poems about that one phenomenon. She'd read, analyzed and taught from countless novels where love was the catalyst to all action, all emotion. With her students, she'd dissected innumerable lines from books, plays and verse that all led back to that one word.

Now, for perhaps the first time in her life, it was offered to her. She found it had more power than could possibly be taught. She found she didn't understand it.

Ky hadn't Byron's way with words, or Keat's romantic phrasing. What he'd said, he'd said simply. It meant everything. She still didn't understand it.

She could, in her own way, understand her feelings. She'd loved Ky for years, since that first revelation one summer when she'd come to know what it meant to want to fully share oneself with another.

But what, she wondered, did Ky find in her to love? It wasn't modesty that caused her to ask herself this question, but the basic practicality she'd grown up with. Where there was an effect, there was a cause. Where there was reaction, there was action. The world ran on this principle. She'd won Ky's love—but how?

Kate had no insecurity about her own intelligence. Perhaps, if anything, she overrated her mind, and it was this that caused her to underrate her other attributes.

He was a man of action, of restless and mercurial nature. She, on the other hand, considered herself almost blandly level. While she thrived on routine, Ky thrived on the unexpected. Why should he love her? Yet he did.

If she accepted that, it was vital to come to a resolution. Love led to commitment. It was there that she found the wall solid, without footholds.

He lived on a remote island because he was basically a loner, because he preferred moving at his own pace, in his own time. She was a teacher who lived by a day-to-day schedule. Without the satisfaction of giving knowledge, she'd stagnate. In the structured routine of a college town, Ky would go mad.

Because she could find no compromise, Kate opted to do what she'd decided to do in the beginning. She'd ride with the current until the summer was over. Perhaps by then, an answer would come.

They spoke no more of percentages. Kate quietly dropped the notion of keeping her hotel room. These, she told herself, were small matters when so much more hung in the balance during her second summer with Ky.

The days went quickly with her and Ky working together with the prop-wash or by hand. Slowly, painstakingly, they uncovered more salvage. The candlesticks had turned out to be pewter, but the coin had been Spanish silver. Its date had been 1748.

In the next two-week period, they uncovered much more—a heavy intricately carved silver platter, more china and porcelain, and in another area dozens of nails and tools.

Kate documented each find on film, for practical and personal reasons. She needed the neat, orderly way of keeping track of the salvage. She wanted to be able to look back on those pictures and remember how she felt when Ky held up a crusted teacup or an oxidized tankard. She'd be able to look and remember how he'd played an outstaring game with a large lazy bluefish. And lost.

More than once Ky had suggested the use of a larger ship equipped for salvage. They discussed it, and its advantages, but they never acted on it. Somehow, they both felt they wanted to move slowly, working basically with their own hands until there came a time when they had to make a decision.

The cannons and the heavier pieces of ship's planking couldn't be brought up without help, so these they left to the sea for the time being. They continued to use tanks, rather than changing to a surface-supplied source of air, so they had to surface and change gear every hour or so. A diving rig would have saved time—but that wasn't their goal.

Their methods weren't efficient by professional salvor standards, but they had an unspoken agreement. Stretch time. Make it last.

The nights they spent together in the big four-poster, talking of the day's finds, or of tomorrow's, making love, marking time. They didn't speak of the future that loomed after the summer's end. They never talked of what they'd do the day after the treasure was found.

The treasure became their focus, something that kept them from reaching out when the other wasn't ready.

The day was fiercely hot as they prepared to dive. The sun was baking. It was mid-July. She'd been in Ocracoke for a month. For all her practicality, Kate told herself it was an omen. Today was the turning point of summer.

Even as she pulled the wet suit up to her waist, sweat beaded on her back. She could almost taste the cool freshness of the water. The sun glared on her tanks as she lifted them, bouncing off to spear her eyes.

"Here." Taking them from her, Ky strapped them onto her back, checking the gauges himself. "The water's going to feel like heaven."

"Yeah." Marsh tipped up a quart bottle of juice. "Think of me baking up here while you're having all the fun."

"Keep the throttle low, brother," Ky said with a grin as he climbed over the side. "We'll bring you a reward."

"Make it something round and shiny with a date stamped on it," Marsh called back, then winked at Kate as she started down the ladder. "Good luck."

She felt the excitement as the water lapped over her ankles. "Today, I don't think I need it."

The noise of the prop-wash disturbed the silence of the water, but not the mystery. Even with technology and equipment, the water remained an enigma, part beauty, part danger. They went deeper and deeper until they reached the site with the scoops in the silt caused by their earlier explorations.

They'd already found what they thought had been the officer's and passenger's quarters, identifying it by the discovery of a snuff box, a silver bedside candleholder and Ky's personal favorite—a decorated sword. The few pieces of jewelry they'd found indicated a personal cache rather than cargo.

Though they fully intended to excavate in the area of the cache, it was the cargo they sought. Using the passenger's quarters and the galley as points of reference, they concentrated on what should have been the stern of the ship.

There were ballast rocks to deal with. This entailed a slow, menial process that required moving them by hand to an area they'd already excavated. It was time consuming, unrewarding and necessary. Still, Kate found something peaceful in the mindless work, and something fascinating about the ability to do it under fathoms of water with basically little effort. She could move a ballast pile as easily as Ky, whereas on land, she would have tired quickly.

Reaching down to clear another area, Ky's fingers brushed something small and hard. Curious, he fanned aside a thin layer of silt and picked up what at first looked like a tab on a can of beer. As he brought it closer, he saw it was much more refined, and though there were layers of crust on the knob of the circle, he felt his heart give a quick jerk.

He'd heard of diamonds in the rough, but he'd never thought to find one by simply reaching for it. He was no expert, but as he painstakingly cleaned what he could from the stone, he judged it to be at least two carats. With a tap on Kate's shoulder, he got her attention.

It gave him a great deal of pleasure to see her eyes widen and to hear the muffled sound of her surprise. Together, they turned it over and over again. It was dull and dirty, but the gem was there.

They were finding bits and pieces of civilization. Perhaps a woman had worn the ring while dining with the captain on her way to America. Perhaps some British officer had carried it in his vest pocket, waiting to give it to the woman he'd hoped to marry. It might have belonged to an elderly widow, or a young bride. The mystery of it, and its tangibility, were more precious than the stone itself. It was...lasting.

Ky held it out to her, offering. Their routine had fallen into a finders-keepers arrangement, in that whoever found a particular piece carried it in their own bag to the surface where everything was carefully catalogued on film and paper. Kate looked at the small, water-dulled piece of the past in Ky's fingers.

Was he offering her the ring because it was a woman's fancy, or was he offering her something else? Unsure, she shook her head, pointing to the bag on his belt. If he were asking her something, she needed it to be done with words.

Ky dropped the ring into his bag, secured it, then went back to work.

He thought he understood her, in some ways. In other ways, Ky found she was as much a mystery as the sea. What did she want from him? If it was love, he'd given her that. If it was time, they were both running out of it. He wanted to demand, was accustomed to demanding, yet she blocked his ability with a look.

She said she'd changed—that she was just beginning to feel in control of her life. He thought he understood that, as well as her fierce need for independence. And yet . . . He'd never known anything but independence. He, too, had changed. He needed her to give him the boundaries and the borders that came with dependence. His for her, and hers for him. Was the timing wrong again? Would it ever be right?

Damn it, he wanted her, he thought as he heaved another rock out of his way. Not just for today, but for tomorrow. Not tied against him, but bound to him. Why couldn't she understand that?

She loved him. It was something she murmured in the night when she was sleepy and caught close against him. She wasn't a woman to use words unless they had meaning. Yet with the love he offered and the love she returned, she'd begun to hold something back from him, as though he could have only a portion of her, but not all.

Edged with frustration, he cleared more ballast. He needed and would have, all.

Marriage? Was he thinking of marriage? Kate found herself flustered and uneasy. She'd never expected Ky to look for that kind of commitment, that kind of permanency. Perhaps she'd misread him. After all, it was difficult to be certain of someone's intention, yet she knew just how clearly Ky and she had been able to communicate underwater.

There was so much to consider, so many things to weigh. He wouldn't understand that, Kate mused. Ky was a man who made decisions in an instant and took the consequences. He wouldn't think about all the variables, all the what-ifs, all the maybes. She had to think about them all. She simply knew no other way.

Kate watched the silt and sand blowing away, causing a cuplike indentation to form on the ocean floor. Outside influences, she mused. They could eat away at the layers and uncover the core, but sometimes what was beneath couldn't stand up to the pressure.

Is that what would happen between she and Ky? How would their relationship hold up under the pressure of variant life-styles—the demands of her profession and the free-wheeling tone of his? Would it stay intact, or would it begin to sift away, layer by layer? How much of herself would he ask her to give? And in loving, how much of herself would she lose?

It was a possibility she couldn't ignore, a threat she needed to build a solid defense against. Time. Perhaps time was the answer. But summer was waning.

The force of the wash made a small object spin up, out of the layer of silt and into the water. Kate grabbed at it and the sharp edge scraped her palm. Curious, she turned it over for examination. A buckle? she wondered. The shape seemed to indicate it, and she could just make out a fastening. Even as she started to hold it out for Ky another, then another was pushed off the ocean bed.

Shoe buckles, Kate realized, astonished. Dozens of them. No, she realized as more and more began to twist up in the water's spin and reel away. Hundreds. With a quick frenzy, she began to gather what she could. More than hundreds, she discovered as her heart thudded. There were thousands of them, literally thousands.

She held a buckle in her hand and looked at Ky in triumph. They'd found the cargo. There'd been shoe buckles on the manifest of the *Liberty*. Five thousand of them. Nothing but a merchantman carried something like that in bulk.

Proof. She waved the buckle, her arm sweeping out in slow motion to take in the swarm of them swirling away from the wash and dropping again. Proof, her mind shouted out. The cargo-hold was beneath them. And the treasure. They had only to reach it.

Ky took her hands and nodded, knowing what was in her mind. Beneath his fingers he could feel the race of her pulse. He wanted that for her, the excitement, the thrill that came from discovering something only half believed in. She brought the back of his hand to her cheek, her eyes laughing, buckles spinning around them. Kate wanted to laugh until she was too weak to stand. Five thousand shoe buckles would guide them to a chest of gold.

Kate saw the humor in his eyes and knew Ky's thoughts ran along the same path as hers. He pointed to himself, then thumbs up. With a minimum of signaling, he told Kate that he would surface to tell Marsh to shut off the engines. It was time to work by hand.

Excited, she nodded. She wanted only to begin. Resting near the bottom, Kate watched Ky go up and out of sight. Oddly, she found she needed time alone. She'd shared the heady instant of discovery with Ky, and now she needed to absorb it.

The *Liberty* was beneath her, the ship her father had searched for. The dream he'd kept close, carefully researching, meticulously calculating, but never finding.

Joy and sorrow mixed as she gathered a handful of the buckles and placed them carefully in her bag. For him. In that moment she felt she'd given him everything she'd always needed to.

Carefully, and this time for personal reasons rather than the catalogue, she began to shoot pictures. Years from now, she thought. Years and years from now, she'd look at a snapshot of swirling silt and drifting pieces of metal, and she'd remember. Nothing could ever take that moment of quiet satisfaction from her.

She glanced up at the sudden silence. The wash had stilled. Ky had reached the surface. Silt and the pieces of crusted, decorated metal began to settle again without the agitation of the wash. The sea was a world without sound, without movement.

Kate looked down at the scoop in the ocean floor. They were nearly there. For a moment she was tempted to begin to fan and search by herself, but she'd wait for Ky. They began together, and they'd finish together. Content, she watched for his return.

When Kate saw the movement above her, she started to signal. Her hand froze in place, then her arm, her shoulder and the rest of her body, degree by degree. It came smoothly through the water, sleek and silent. Deadly.

The noise of the prop-wash had kept the sea life away. Now the abrupt quiet brought out the curious. Among the schools of harmless fish glided the long bulletlike shape of a shark.

Kate was still, hardly daring to breathe as she feared even the trail of bubbles might attract him. He moved without haste, apparently not interested in her. Perhaps he'd already hunted successfully that day. But even with a full belly, a shark would attack what annoyed his uncertain temper.

She gauged him to be ten feet in length. Part of her mind registered that he was fairly small for what she recognized as a tiger shark. They could easily double that length. But she knew the jaws, those large sickle-shaped teeth, would be strong, merciless and fatal.

If she remained still, the chances were good that he would simply go in search of more interesting waters. Isn't that what she'd read sitting cozily under lamplight at her own desk? Isn't that what Ky had told her once when they'd shared a quiet lunch on his boat? All that seemed so remote, so unreal now, as she looked above and saw the predator between herself and the surface.

It was movement that attracted them, she reminded herself as she forced her mind to function. The movement a swimmer made with kicking feet and sweeping arms.

Don't panic. She forced herself to breath slowly. No sudden moves. She forced her nervous hands to form tight, still fists.

He was no more than ten feet away. Kate could see the small black eyes and the gentle movement of his gills. Breathing shallowly, she never took her eyes from his. She had only to be perfectly still and wait for him to swim on.

But Ky. Kate's mouth went dry as she looked toward the direction where Ky had disappeared moments before. He'd be coming back, any minute, unaware of what was lurking near the bottom. Waiting. Cruising.

The shark would sense the disturbance in the water with the uncanny ability the hunter had. The kick of Ky's feet, the swing of his arms would attract the shark long before Kate would have a chance to warn him of any danger.

He'd be unaware, helpless, and then... Her blood seemed to freeze. She'd heard of the sensation but now she experienced it. Cold seemed to envelop her. Terror made her head light. Kate bit down on her lip until pain cleared her thoughts. She wouldn't stand by idly while Ky came blindly into a death trap.

Glancing down, she saw the spear gun. It was over five feet away and unloaded for safety. Safety, she thought hysterically. She'd never loaded one, much less shot one. And first, she'd have to get to it. There'd only be one chance. Knowing she'd have no time to settle her nerves, Kate made her move.

She kept her eyes on the shark as she inched slowly toward the gun. At the moment, he seemed to be merely cruising, not particularly interested in anything. He never even glanced her way. Perhaps he would move on before Ky came back, but she needed the weapon. Fingers shaking, she gripped the butt of the gun. Time seemed to crawl. Her movements were so slow, so measured, she hardly seemed to move at all. But her mind whirled.

Even as she gripped the spear she saw the shape that glided down from the surface. The shark turned lazily to the left. To Ky.

No! her mind screamed as she rammed the spear into position. Her only thought that of protecting what she loved. Kate swam forward without hesitation, taking a path between Ky and the shark. She had to get close.

Her mind was cold now, with fear, with purpose. For the second time, she saw those small, deadly eyes. This time, they focused on her. If she'd never seen true evil before, Kate knew she faced it now. This was cruelty, and a death that wouldn't come easily.

The shark moved toward her with a speed that made her heart stop. His jaws opened. There was a black, black cave behind them.

Ky dove quickly, wanting to get back to Kate, wanting to search for what had brought them back together. If it was the treasure she needed to settle her mind, he'd find it. With it, they could open whatever doors they needed to open, lock whatever needed to be locked. Excitement drummed through him as he dove deeper.

When he spotted the shark, he pulled up short. He'd felt that deep primitive fear before, but never so sharply. Though it was less than useless against such a predator, he reached for his diver's knife. He'd left Kate alone. Cold bloodedly, he set for the attack.

Like a rocket, Kate shot up between himself and the shark. Terror such as he'd never known washed over him. Was she mad? Was she simply unaware? Giving no time to thought, Ky barreled through the water toward her.

He was too far away. He knew it even as the panic hammered into him. The shark would be on her before he was close enough to sink the knife in.

When he saw what she held in her hand, and realized her purpose he somehow doubled his speed. Everything was in slow motion, and yet it seemed to happen in the blink of eye. He saw the gaping hole in the shark's mouth as it closed in on Kate. For the first time in his life, prayers ran through him like water.

The spear shot out, sinking deep through the shark's flesh. Instinctively, Kate let herself drop as the shark came forward full of anger and pain. He would follow her now, she knew. If the spear didn't work, he would be on her in moments.

Ky saw blood gush from the wound. It wouldn't be enough. The shark jerked as if to reject the spear, and slowed his pace. Just enough. Teeth bared, Ky fell on its back, hacking with the knife as quickly as the water would allow. The shark turned, furious. Using all his strength, Ky turned with it, forcing the knife into the underbelly and ripping down. It ran through his mind that he was holding death, and it was as cold as the poets said.

From a few feet away, Kate watched the battle. She was numb, body and mind. Blood spurted out to dissipate in the water. Letting the empty gun fall, she too reached for her knife and swam forward.

But it was over. One instant the fish and Ky were as one form, locked together. Then they were separate as the body of the shark sank lifelessly toward the bottom. She saw the eyes one last time.

Her arm was gripped painfully. Limp, Kate allowed herself to be dragged to the surface. Safe. It was the only clear thought her mind could form. He was safe.

Too breathless to speak, Ky pulled her toward the ladder, tanks and all. He saw her slip near the top and roll onto the deck. Even as he swung over himself, he saw two fins slice through the water and disappear below where the blood drew them.

"What the hell—" Jumping up from his seat, Marsh ran across the deck to where Kate still lay, gasping for air.

"Sharks." Ky cut off the word as he knelt beside her. "I had to bring her up fast. Kate." Ky reached a hand beneath her neck, lifting her up as he began to take off her tanks. "Are you dizzy? Do you have any pain—your knees, elbows?"

Though she was still gasping for air, she shook her head. "No, no, I'm all right." She knew he worried about decompression sickness and tried to steady herself to reassure him. "Ky, we weren't that deep after—when we came up."

He nodded, grimly acknowledging that she was winded, not incoherent. Standing, he pulled off his mask and heaved it across the deck. Temper helped alleviate the helpless shaking. Kate merely drew her knees up and rested her forehead on them.

"Somebody want to fill me in?" Marsh asked, glancing from one to the other. "I left off when Ky came up raving about shoe buckles."

"Cargo-hold," Kate murmured. "We found it."

"So Ky said." Marsh glanced at his brother whose knuckles were whitening against the rail as he looked out to sea. "Run into some company down there?"

"There was a shark. A tiger."

"She nearly got herself killed," Ky explained. Fury was a direct result of fear, and just as deadly. "She swam right in front of him." Before Marsh could make any comment, Ky turned on Kate. "Did you forget everything I taught you?" he demanded. "You manage to get a doctorate but you can't remember that you're supposed to minimize your movements when a shark's cruising? You know that arm and leg swings attract them, but you swim in front of him, flailing around as though you wanted to shake hands—holding a damn spear gun that's just as likely to annoy him as do any real damage. If I hadn't been coming down just then, he'd have torn you to pieces."

Kate lifted her head slowly. Whatever emotion she'd felt up to that moment was replaced by an anger so deep it overshadowed everything. Meticulously she removed her flippers, her mask and her weight belt before she rose. "If you hadn't been coming down just then," she said precisely, "there'd have been no reason for me to swim in front of him." Turning, she walked to the steps and down into the cabin.

For a full minute there was utter silence on deck. Above, a gull screeched, then swerved west. Knowing there'd be no more dives that day, Marsh went to the helm. As he glanced over he saw the deep stain of blood on the water's surface.

"It's customary," he began with his back to his brother, "to thank someone when they save your life." Without waiting for a comment, he switched on the engine.

Shaken, Ky ran a hand through his hair. Some of the shark's blood had stained his fingers. Standing still, he stared at it.

Not through carelessness, he thought with a jolt. It had been deliberate. Kate had deliberately put herself in the path of the shark. For him. She'd risked her life to save him. He ran both hands over his face before he started below deck.

He saw her sitting on a bunk with a glass in her hand. A bottle of brandy sat at her feet. When she lifted the glass to her lips her hand shook lightly. Beneath the tan the sun had given her, her face was drawn and pale. No one had ever put him first so completely, so unselfishly. It left him without any idea of what to say.

"Kate..."

"I'm not in the mood to be shouted at right now," she told him before she drank again. "If you need to vent your temper, you'll have to save it."

"I'm not going to shout." Because he felt every bit as unsteady as she did, he sat beside her and lifted the bottle, drinking straight from it. The brandy ran hot and strong through him. "You scared the hell out of me."

"I'm not going to apologize for what I did."

"I should thank you." He drank again and felt the nerves in his stomach ease. "The point is, you had no business doing what you did. Nothing but blind luck kept you from being torn up down there."

Turning her head, she stared at him. "I should've stayed safe and sound on the bottom while you dealt with the shark—with your diver's knife."

He met the look levelly. "Yes."

"And you'd have done that, if it'd been me?"

"That's different."

"Oh." Glass in hand, she rose. She took a moment to study him, that raw-boned, dark face, the dripping hair that needed a trim, the eyes that reflected the sea. "Would you care to explain that little piece of logic to me?"

"I don't have to explain it, it just is." He tipped the bottle back again. It helped to cloud his imagination which kept bringing images of what might have happened to her.

"No, it just isn't, and that's one of your major problems."

"Kate, have you any idea what could have happened if you hadn't lucked out and hit a vital spot with that spear?"

"Yes." She drained her glass and felt some of the edge dull. The fear might come back again unexpectedly, but she felt she was strong enough to deal with it. And the anger. No matter how it slashed at her, she would put herself between him and danger again. "I understand perfectly. Now, I'm going up with Marsh."

"Wait a minute." He stood to block her way. "Can't you see that I couldn't stand it if anything happened to you? I want to take care of you. I need to keep you safe."

"While you take all the risks?" she countered. "Is that supposed to be the balance of our relationship, Ky? You man, me woman? I bake bread, you hunt the meat?"

"Damn it, Kate, it's not as basic as that."

"It's just as basic as that," she tossed back. The color had come back to her face. Her legs were steady again. And she would be heard. "You want me to be quiet and content—and amenable to the way you choose to live. You want me to do as you say, bend to your will, and yet I know how you felt about my father."

It didn't seem she had the energy to be angry any longer. She was just weary, bone weary from slamming herself up against a wall that didn't seem ready to budge.

"I spent all my life doing what it pleased him to have me do," she continued in calmer tones. "No waves, no problems, no rebellion. He gave me a nod of approval, but no true respect and certainly no true affection. Now, you're asking me to do the same thing again with you." She felt no tears, only that weariness of spirit. "Why do you suppose the only two men I've ever loved should want me to be so utterly pliant to their will? Why do you suppose I lost both of them because I tried so hard to do just that?"

"No." He put his hands on her shoulders. "No, that's not true. It's not what I want from you or for you. I just want to take care of you."

She shook her head. "What's the difference, Ky?" she whispered. "What the hell's the difference?" Pushing past him, Kate went out on deck.

# Chapter Twelve

Because in her quiet, immovable way Kate had demanded it, Ky left her alone. Perhaps it was for the best as it gave him time to think and to reassess what he wanted.

He realized that because of his fear for her, because of his need to care for her, he'd hurt her and damaged their already tenuous relationship.

On a certain level, she'd hit the mark in her accusations. He did want her to be safe and cared for while he sweated and took the risks. It was his nature to protect what he loved—in Kate's case, perhaps too much. It was also his nature to want other wills bent to his. He wanted Kate, and was honest enough to admit that he'd already outlined the terms in his own mind.

Her father's quiet manipulating had infuriated Ky and yet, he found himself doing the same thing. Not so quietly, he admitted, not nearly as subtly, but he was doing the same thing. Still, it wasn't for the same reasons. He wanted Kate to be with him, to align herself to him. It was as simple as that. He was certain, if she'd just let him, that he could make her happy.

But he never fully considered that she'd have demands or terms of her own. Until now, Ky hadn't thought how he'd adjust to them.

The light of dawn was quiet as Ky added the finishing touches to the lettering on his sailboat. For most of the night, he'd worked in the shed, giving Kate her time alone, and himself the time to think. Now that the night was over, only one thing remained clear. He loved her. But it had come home to him that it might not be enough. Though impatience continued to push at him, he reined it in. Perhaps he had to leave it to her to show him what would be.

For the next few days, they would concentrate on excavating the cargo that had sunk two centuries before. The longer they searched, the more the treasure became a symbol for him. If he could give it to her, it would be the end of the quest for both of them. Once it was over, they'd both have what they wanted. She, the fulfillment of her father's dream, and he, the satisfaction of seeing her freed from it.

Ky closed the shed doors behind him and headed back for the house. In a few days, he thought with a glance over his shoulder, he'd have something else to give her. Something else to ask her.

He was still some feet away from the house when he smelled the morning scents of bacon and coffee drifting through the kitchen windows. When he entered, Kate was standing at the stove, a long T-shirt over her tank suit, her feet bare, her hair loose. He could see the light dusting of freckles over the bridge of her nose, and the pale soft curve of her lips.

His need to gather her close rammed into him with such power, he had to stop and catch his breath. "Kate—"

"I thought since we'd be putting in a long day we should have a full breakfast." She'd heard him come in, sensed it. Because it made her knees weak, she spoke briskly. "I'd like to get an early start."

He watched her drop eggs into the skillet where the white began to sizzle and solidify around the edges. "Kate, I'd like to talk to you."

"I've been thinking we might consider renting a salvage ship after all," she interrupted, "and perhaps hiring another couple of divers. Excavating the cargo's going to be very slow work with just the two of us. It's certainly time we looked into lifting bags and lines."

Long days in the sun had lightened her hair. There were shades upon shades of variation so that as it flowed it reminded him of the smooth soft pelt of a deer. "I don't want to talk business now."

"It's not something we can put off too much longer." Efficiently, she scooped up the eggs and slid them onto plates. "I'm beginning to think we should expedite the excavation rather than dragging it out for what may very well be several more weeks. Then, of course, if we're talking about excavating the entire site, it would be months."

"Not now." Ky turned off the burner under the skillet. Taking both plates from Kate, he set them on the table. "Look, I have to do something, and I'm not sure I'll do it very well."

Turning, Kate took silverware from the drawer and went to the table. "What?"

"Apologize." When she looked back at him in her cool, quiet way, he swore. "No, I won't do it well."

"It isn't necessary."

"Yes, it's necessary. Sit down." He let out a long breath as she remained standing. "Please," he added, then took a chair himself. Without a word, Kate sat across from him. "You saved my life yesterday." Even saying it aloud, he felt uneasy about it. "It was no less than that. I never could have taken that shark with my diver's knife. The only reason I did was because you'd weakened and distracted him."

Kate lifted her coffee and drank as though they were discussing the weather. It was the only way she had of blocking out images of what might have been. "Yes."

With a frustrated laugh, Ky stabbed at his eggs. "Not going to make it easy on me, are you?"

"No, I don't think I am."

"I've never been that scared," he said quietly. "Not for myself, certainly not for anyone else. I thought he had you." He looked up and met her calm, patient eyes. "I was still too far away to do anything about it. If . . ."

"Sometimes it's best not to think about the ifs."

"All right." He nodded and reached for her hand. "Kate, realizing you put yourself in danger to protect me only made it worse somehow. The possibility of anything happening to you was bad enough, but the idea of it happening because of me was unbearable."

"You would've protected me."

"Yes, but—"

"There shouldn't be any buts, Ky."

"Maybe there shouldn't be," he agreed, "but I can't promise there won't be."

"I've changed." The fact filled her with an odd sense of power and unease. "For too many years I've channeled my own desires because I thought somehow that approval could be equated with love. I know better now."

"I'm not your father, Kate."

"No, but you also have a way of imposing your will on me. My fault to a point." Her voice was calm, level, as it was when she lectured her students. She hadn't slept while Ky had spent his hours in the shed. Like him, she'd spent her time in thought, in search for the right answers. "Four years ago, I had to give to one of you and deny the other. It broke my heart. Today, I know I have to answer to myself first.'' With her breakfast hardly touched, she took her plate to the sink. ''I love you, Ky,'' she murmured. ''But I have to answer to myself first.''

Rising, he went to her and laid his hands on her shoulders. Somehow the strength that suddenly seemed so powerful in her both attracted him yet left him uneasy. ''Okay.'' When she turned into his arms, he felt the world settle a bit. ''Just let me know what the answer is.''

''When I can.'' She closed her eyes and held tight. ''When I can.''

For three long days they dove, working away the silt to find new discoveries. With a small air lift and their own hands, they found the practical, the beautiful and the ordinary. They came upon more than eight thousand of the ten thousand decorated pipes on the *Liberty*'s manifest. At least half of them, to Kate's delight, had their bowls intact. They were clay, long-stemmed pipes with the bowls decorated with oak leaves or bunches of grapes and flowers. In a heady moment of pleasure, she snapped Ky's picture as he held one up to his lips.

She knew that at auction, they would more than pay for the investment she'd made. And, with them, the donation she'd make to a museum in her father's name was steadily growing. But more than this, the discovery of so many pipes on a wreck added force to their claim that the ship was English.

There were also snuff boxes, again thousands, leaving literally no doubt in her mind that they'd found the merchantman *Liberty*. They found tableware, some of it elegant, some basic utility-ware, but again in quantity. Their list of salvage grew beyond anything Kate had imagined, but they found no chest of gold.

They took turns hauling their finds to the surface, using an inverted plastic trash can filled with air to help them lift. Even with this, they stored the bulk of it on the sea floor. They were working alone again, without a need for Marsh to man the prop-wash. As it had been in the beginning, the project became a personal chore for only the two of them. What they found became a personal triumph. What they didn't find, a personal disappointment.

Kate delegated herself to deal with the snuff boxes, transporting them to the mesh baskets. Already, she was planning to clean several of them herself as part of the discovery. Beneath the layers of time there might be something elegant, ornate or ugly. She didn't believe it mattered what she found, as long as she found it.

Tea, sugar and other perishables the merchant ship had carried were long since gone without a trace. What she and Ky found now were the solid pieces of civilization that had survived centuries in the sea. A pipe meant for an eighteenth-century man had never reached the New World. It should have made her sad but, because it had survived, because she could hold it in her hand more than two hundred years later, Kate felt a quiet triumph. Some things last, whatever the odds.

Reaching down, she disturbed something that lay among the jumbled snuff boxes. Automatically, she jerked her hand back. Memories of the stingray and other dangers were still very fresh. When the small round object clinked against the side of a box and lay still, her heart began to pound. Almost afraid to touch, Kate reached for it. Between her fingers, she held a gold coin from another era.

Though she had read it was likely, she hadn't expected it to be as bright and shiny as the day it was minted. The pieces of silver they'd found had blackened, and other metal pieces had corroded, some of them crystalized almost beyond recognition. Yet, the gold, the small coin she'd plucked from the sea floor, winked back at her.

Its origin was English. The long-dead king stared out at her. The date was 1750.

Ky! Foolishly, she said his name. Though the sound was muffled and indistinguishable, he turned. Unable to wait, Kate swam toward him, clutching the coin. When she reached him, she took his hand and pressed the gold into his palm.

He knew at the moment of contact. He had only to look into her eyes. Taking her hand, he brought it to his lips. She'd found what she wanted. For no reason he could name, he felt empty. He pressed the coin back into her hand, closing her fingers over it tightly. The gold was hers.

Swimming beside her, Ky moved to the spot where Kate had found the coin. Together, they fanned, using all the patience each of them had stored. In the twenty minutes of bottom time they had left, they uncovered only five more coins. As if they were as fragile as glass, Kate placed them in her bag. Each took a mesh basket filled with salvage and surfaced.

"It's there, Ky." Kate let her mouthpiece drop as Ky hauled the first basket over the rail. "It's the *Liberty*, we've proven it."

"It's the *Liberty*," he agreed, taking the second basket from her. "You've finished what your father started."

"Yes." She unhooked her tanks, but it was more than their weight she felt lifted from her shoulders. "I've finished." Digging into her bag, she pulled out the six bright coins. "These were loose. We still haven't found the chest. If it still exists."

He'd already thought of that, but not how he'd tell her his own theory. "They might have taken the chest to another part of the boat when the storm hit." It was a possibility; it had given them hope that the chest was still there.

Kate looked down. The glittery metal seemed to mock her. "It's possible they put the gold in one of the lifeboats when they manned them. The survivor's story wasn't clear after the ship began to break up."

"A lot of things are possible." He touched her cheek briefly before he started to strip off his gear. "With a little luck and a little more time, we might find it all."

She smiled as she dropped the coins back into her bag. "Then you could buy your boat."

"And you could go to Greece." Stripped down to his bathing trunks, Ky went to the helm. "We need to give ourselves the full twelve hours before we dive again, Kate. We've been calling it close as it is."

"That's fine." She made a business of removing her own suit. She needed the twelve hours, she discovered, for more than the practical reason of residual nitrogen.

They spoke little on the trip back. They should've been ecstatic. Kate knew it, and though she tried, she couldn't recapture that quick boost she'd felt when she picked up the first coin.

She discovered that if she'd had a choice she would have gone back weeks, to the time when the gold was a distant goal and the search was everything.

It took the rest of the day to transport the salvage from the *Vortex* to Ky's house, to separate and catalog it. She'd already decided to contact the Park Service. Their advice in placing many of the artifacts would be invaluable. After taxes, she'd give her father his memorial. And, she mused, she'd give Ky whatever he wanted out of the salvage.

Their original agreement no longer mattered to her. If he wanted half, she'd give it. All she wanted, Kate realized, was the first bowl she'd found, the blackened silver coin and the gold one that had led her to the five other coins.

"We might think about investing in a small electrolytic reduction bath," Ky murmured as he turned what he guessed was a silver snuff box in his palm. "We could treat a lot of this salvage ourselves." Coming to a decision, he set the box down. "We're going to have to think about a bigger ship and equipment. It might be best to stop diving for the next couple of days while we arrange for it. It's been six weeks, and we've barely scratched the surface of what's down there."

She nodded, not entirely sure why she wanted to weep. He was right. It was time to move on, to expand. How could she explain to him, when she couldn't explain to herself, that she wanted nothing else from the sea? While the sun set, she watched him meticulously list the salvage.

"Ky..." She broke off because she couldn't find the words to tell him what moved through her. Sadness, emptiness, needs.

"What's wrong?"

"Nothing." But she took his hands as she rose. "Come upstairs now," she said quietly. "Make love with me before the sun goes down."

Questions ran through him, but he told himself they could wait. The need he felt from her touched off his own. He wanted to give her, and to take from her, what couldn't be found anywhere else.

When they entered the bedroom it was washed with the warm, lingering light of the sun. The sky was slowly turning red as he lay beside her. Her arms reached out to gather him close. Her lips parted. Refusing to rush, they undressed each other. No boundaries. Flesh against flesh they lay. Mouth against mouth they touched.

Kisses—long and deep—took them both beyond the ordinary world of place and time. Here, there were dozens of sensations to be felt, and no questions to be asked. Here, there was no past, no tomorrow, only the moment. Her body went limp under his, but her mouth hungered and sought.

No one else . . . No one else had ever taken her beyond herself so effortlessly. Never before had anyone made her so completely aware of her own body. A feathery touch along her skin drove pleasure through her with inescapable force.

The scent of sea still clung to both of them. As pleasure became liquid, they might have been fathoms under the ocean, moving freely without the strict rules of gravity. There were no rules here.

As his hands brought their emotions rising to the surface, so did hers for him. She explored the rippling muscles of his back, near the shoulders. Lingering there, she enjoyed just the feel of one of the subtle differences between them. His skin was smooth, but muscles bunched under it. His hands were gentle, but the palms were hard. He was lean, but there was no softness there.

Again and again she touched and tasted, needing to absorb him. Above all else, she needed to experience everything they'd ever had together this one time. They made love here, she remembered, that first time. The first time...and the last. Whenever she thought of him, she'd remember the quieting light of dusk and the distant sound of surf.

He didn't understand why he felt such restrained urgency from her, but he knew she needed everything he could give her. He loved her, perhaps not as gently as he could, but more thoroughly than ever before.

He touched. "Here," Ky murmured, using his fingertips to drive her up. As she gasped and arched, he watched her. "You're soft and hot."

He tasted. "And here . . ." With his tongue, he pushed her to the edge. As her hands gripped his, he groaned. Pleasure heaped upon pleasure. "You taste like temptation—sweet and forbidden. Tell me you want more."

"Yes." The word came out on a moan. "I want more."

So he gave her more.

Again and again, he took her up, watching the astonished pleasure on her face, feeling it in the arch of her body, hearing it in her quick breaths. She was helpless, mindless, his. He drove his tongue into her and felt her explode, wave after wave.

As she shuddered, he moved up her body, hands fast, mouth hot and open. Suddenly, on a surge of strength, she rolled on top of him. Within seconds, she'd devastated his claim to leadership. All fire, all speed, all woman, she took control.

Heedless, greedy, they moved over the bed. Murmurs were incoherent, care was forgotten. They took with only one goal in mind. Pleasure—sweet, forbidden pleasure.

Shaking, locked tight, they reached the goal together.

Dawn was breaking, clear and calm as Kate lay still, watching Ky sleep. She knew what she had to do for both of them, to both of them. Fate had brought them together a second time. It wouldn't bring them together again.

She'd bargained with Ky, offering him a share of gold for his skill. In the beginning, she'd believed that she wanted the treasure, needed it to give her all the options she'd never had before. That choice. Now, she knew she didn't want it at all. A hundred times more gold wouldn't change what was between her and Ky—what drew them to each other, and what kept them apart.

She loved him. She understood that, in his way, he loved her. Did that change the differences between them? Did that make her able and willing to give up her own life to suit his, or able and willing to demand that he do the same?

Their worlds were no closer together now than they'd been four years ago. Their desires no more in tune. With the gold she'd leave for him, he'd be able to do what he wanted with his life. She needed no treasure for that.

If she stayed... Unable to stop herself, Kate reached out to touch his cheek. If she stayed she'd bury herself for him. Eventually, she'd despise herself for it, and he'd resent her. Better that they take what they'd had for a few weeks than cover it with years of disappoinments.

The treasure was important to him. He'd taken risks for it, worked for it. She'd give her father his memorial. Ky would have the rest.

Quietly, still watching him sleep, she dressed.

It didn't take Kate long to gather what she'd come with. Taking her suitcase downstairs, she carefully packed what she'd taken with her from the *Liberty*. In a box, she placed the pottery bowl wrapped in layers of newspaper. The coins, the blackened silver and the shiny gold she zipped into a small pouch. With equal care, she packed the film she'd taken during their days under the ocean.

What she'd designated for the museum she'd already marked. Leaving the list on the table, she left the house.

She told herself it would be cleaner if she left no note, yet she found herself hesitating. How could she make him understand? After putting her suitcase in her car, she went back into the house. Quietly, she took the five gold coins upstairs and placed them on Ky's dresser. With a last look at him as he slept, she went back out again.

She'd have a final moment with the sea. In the quiet air of morning, Kate walked over the dunes.

She'd remember it this way—empty, endless and full of sound. Surf foamed against the sand, white on white. What was beneath the surface would always call her—the memories of peace, of excitement, of sharing both with Ky. Only a summer, she thought. Life was made of four seasons, not one.

Day was strengthening, and her time was up. Turning, she scanned the island until she saw the tip of the lighthouse. Some things lasted, she thought with a smile. She'd learned a great deal in a few short weeks. She was her own woman at last. She could make her own way. As a teacher, she told herself that knowledge was precious. But it made her ache with loneliness. She left the empty sea behind her.

Though she wanted to, Kate deliberately kept herself from looking at the house as she walked back to her car. She didn't need to see it again to remember it. If things had been different . . . Kate reached for the door handle of her car. Her fingers were still inches from it when she was spun around.

"What the hell're you doing?"

Facing Ky, she felt her resolve crumble, then rebuild. He was barely awake, and barely dressed. His eyes were heavy with sleep, his hair disheveled from it. All he wore was a pair of ragged cut-offs. She folded her hands in front of her and hoped her voice would be strong and clear.

"I had hoped to be gone before you woke."

"Gone?" His eyes locked on hers. "Where?"

"I'm going back to Connecticut."

"Oh?" He swore he wouldn't lose his temper. Not this time. This time, it might be fatal for both of them. "Why?"

Her nerves skipped. The question had been quiet enough, but she knew that cold, flat expression in his eyes. The wrong move, and he'd leap. "You said it yourself yesterday, Ky, when we came up from the last dive. I've done what I came for."

He opened his hand. Five coins shone in the morning sun. "What about this?"

"I left them for you." She swallowed, no longer certain how long she could speak without showing she was breaking in two. "The treasure isn't important to me. It's yours."

"Damn generous of you." Turning over his hand, he dropped the coins into the sand. "That's how much the gold means to me, professor."

She stared at the gold on the ground in front of her. "I don't understand you."

"*You* wanted the treasure," he tossed at her. "It never mattered to me."

"But you said," she began, then shook her head. "When I first came to you, you took the job because of the treasure."

"I took the job because of you. You wanted the gold, Kate."

"It wasn't the money." Dragging a hand through her hair, she turned away. "It was never the money."

"Maybe not. It was your father."

She nodded because it was true, but it no longer hurt. "I finished what he started, and I gave myself something. I don't want any more coins, Ky."

"Why are you running away from me again?"

Slowly, she turned back. "We're four years older than we were before, but we're the same people."

"So?"

"Ky, when I went away before, it was partially because of my father, because I felt I owed him my loyalty. But if I'd thought you'd wanted me. *Me*," she repeated, placing her palm over her heart, "not what you wanted me to be. If I'd thought that, and if I'd thought you and I could make a future together, I wouldn't have gone. I wouldn't be leaving now."

"What the hell gives you the right to decide what I want, what I feel?" He whirled away from her, too furious to remain close. "Maybe I made mistakes, maybe I just assumed too much four years ago. Damn it, I paid for it, Kate, every day from the time you left until you came back. I've done everything I could to be careful this time around, not to push, not to assume. Then I wake up and find you leaving without a word."

"There aren't any words, Ky. I've always given you too many of them, and you've never given me enough."

"You're better with words than I am."

"All right, then I'll use them. I love you." She waited until he turned back to her. The restlessness was on him again. He was holding it off with sheer will. "I've always loved you, but I think I know my own limitations. Maybe I know yours too."

"No, you think too much about limitations, Kate, and not enough about possibilities. I let you walk away from me before. It's not going to be so easy this time."

"I have to be my own person, Ky. I won't live the rest of my life as I've lived it up to now."

"Who the hell wants you to?" he exploded. "Who the hell wants you to be anything but what you are? It's about time you stopped equating love with responsibility and started looking at the other side of it. It's sharing, giving and taking and laughing. If I ask you to give part of yourself to me, I'm going to give part of myself right back."

Unable to stop himself he took her arms in his hands, just holding, as if through the contact he could make his words sink in.

"I don't want your constant devotion. I don't want you to be obliged to me. I don't want to go through life thinking that whatever you do, you do because you want to please me. Damn it, I don't want that kind of responsibility."

Without words, she stared at him. He'd never said anything to her so simply, so free of half meanings. Hope rose in her. Yet still, he was telling her only what he didn't want. Once he gave her the flip side of that coin hope could vanish.

"Tell me what you do want."

He had only one answer. "Come with me a minute." Taking her hand, he drew her toward the shed. "When I started this, it was because I'd always promised myself I would. Before long, the reasons changed." Turning the latch, he pulled the shed doors open.

For a moment, she saw nothing. Gradually, her eyes adjusted to the dimness and she stepped inside. The boat was nearly finished. The hull was sanded and sealed and painted, waiting for Ky to take it outside and attach the mast. It was lovely, clean and simple. Just looking at it, Kate could imagine the way it would flow with the wind. Free, light and clever.

"It's beautiful, Ky. I always wondered..." She broke off as she read the name printed boldly on the stern.

Second Chance.

"That's all I want from you," Ky told her, pointing to the two words. "The boat's yours. When I started it, I thought I was building it for me. But I built it for you, because I knew it was one dream you'd share with me. I only want what's printed on it, Kate. For both of us." Speechless, she watched him lean over the starboard side and open a small compartment. He drew out a tiny box.

"I had this cleaned. You wouldn't take it from me before." Opening the lid, he revealed the diamond he'd found, sparkling now in a simple gold setting. "It didn't cost me anything and it wasn't made especially for you. It's just something I found among a bunch of rocks."

When she started to speak, he held up a hand. "Hold on. You wanted words, I haven't finished with them yet. I know you have to teach, I'm not asking you to give it up. I am asking that you give me one year here on the island. There's a school here, not Yale, but people still have to be taught. A year, Kate. If it isn't what you want after that, I'll go back with you."

Her brows drew together. "Back? To Connecticut? You'd live in Connecticut?"

"If that's what it takes."

A compromise...she thought, baffled. Was he offering to adjust his life for hers? "And if that isn't right for you?"

"Then we'll try someplace else, damn it. We'll find some place in between. Maybe we'll move half a dozen times in the next few years. What does it matter?"

What did it matter? she wondered as she studied him. He was offering her what she'd waited for all of her life. Love without chains.

"I want you to marry me." He wondered if that simple statement shook her as much as it did him. "Tomorrow isn't soon enough, but if you'll give me the year, I can wait."

She nearly smiled. He'd never wait. Once he had her promise of the year, he'd subtly and not so subtly work on her until she found herself at the altar. It was nearly tempting to make him go through the effort.

Limitations? Had she spoken of limitations? Love had none.

"No," she decided aloud. "You only get the year if I get the ring. And what goes with it."

"Deal." He took her hand quickly as though she might change her mind. "Once it's on, you're stuck, professor." Pulling the ring from the box he slipped it onto her finger. Swearing lightly, he shook his head. "It's too big."

"It's all right. I'll keep my hand closed for the next fifty years or so." With a laugh, she went into his arms. All doubts vanished. They'd made it, she told herself. South, north or anywhere in between.

"We'll have it sized," he murmured, nuzzling into her neck.

"Only if they can do it while it's on my finger." Kate closed her eyes. She'd just found everything. Did he know it? "Ky, about the *Liberty*, the rest of the treasure."

He tilted her face up to kiss her. "We've already found it."

\* \* \* \* \*

# Take 4 bestselling love stories FREE

## Plus get a FREE surprise gift!

## Special Limited-time Offer

**Mail to Silhouette Reader Service™**

3010 Walden Avenue
P.O. Box 1867
Buffalo, N.Y. 14269-1867

**YES!** Please send me 4 free Silhouette Intimate Moments® novels and my free surprise gift. Then send me 6 brand-new novels every month, which I will receive months before they appear in bookstores. Bill me at the low price of $2.89 each plus 25¢ delivery and applicable sales tax, if any.* That's the complete price and—compared to the cover prices of $3.50 each—quite a bargain! I understand that accepting the books and gift places me under no obligation ever to buy any books. I can always return a shipment and cancel at any time. Even if I never buy another book from Silhouette, the 4 free books and the surprise gift are mine to keep forever.

245 BPA ANRR

| | |
|---|---|
| Name | (PLEASE PRINT) |
| Address | Apt. No. |
| City | State     Zip |

This offer is limited to one order per household and not valid to present Silhouette Intimate Moments® subscribers. *Terms and prices are subject to change without notice. Sales tax applicable in N.Y.

UMOM-94R

©1990 Harlequin Enterprises Limited

## Silhouette

### SPECIAL EDITION™

# Nora Roberts

## CONVINCING ALEX

# Those Wild Ukrainians

### Look who Detective Alex Stanislaski has picked up....

When soap opera writer Bess McNee hit the streets in spandex pants and a clinging tube-top in order to research the role of a prostitute, she was looking for trouble—but not too much trouble.

Then she got busted by straight-laced Detective Alex Stanislaski and found a lot more than she'd bargained for. This man wasn't buying anything she said, and Bess realized she was going to have to be a *lot* more convincing....

If you enjoyed TAMING NATASHA (SE #583), LURING A LADY (SE #709) and FALLING FOR RACHEL (SE #810), then be sure to read CONVINCING ALEX, the delightful tale of another one of THOSE WILD UKRAINIANS finding love where it's least expected.

# SPRING Fancy '94

### They're sexy, single... and about to get snagged!

Passion is in full bloom as love catches the fancy of three brash bachelors. You won't want to miss these stories by three of Silhouette's hottest authors:

**CAIT LONDON
DIXIE BROWNING
PEPPER ADAMS**

Spring fever is in the air this March— and there's no avoiding it!

*Only from*

🔻 *Silhouette*®

*where passion lives.*

SF94

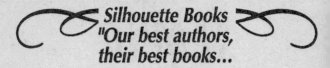

## Silhouette Books
### "Our best authors, their best books...

**DIANA PALMER**
*Soldier of Fortune* in February

**ELIZABETH LOWELL**
*Dark Fire* in February

**LINDA LAEL MILLER**
*Ragged Rainbow* in March

**JOAN HOHL**
*California Copper* in March

**LINDA HOWARD**
*An Independent Wife* in April

**HEATHER GRAHAM POZZESSERE**
*Double Entendre* in April

### When it comes to passion, we wrote the book.

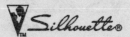

BOBQ1